FOR

Bree wasn't baby Ben's mother; her
sister Briony was, but Briony hadn't
wanted him, and had callously abandoned him. But no way was Bree going
to let him go. And if the forceful Heath
Durant had an even stronger claim on
the baby—well, it was up to Bree to
fight him . . .!

Books you will enjoy
by LYNSEY STEVENS

CLOSEST PLACE TO HEAVEN

Kezia McCoy had had a crush on Shann Evans for years, and it was a shock when she was forced to realise just how much she had been wasting her time. She had fallen in love with one man who didn't take her seriously—and she wasn't going to make the same mistake twice . . .

MAN OF VENGEANCE

Rohan Wilding was back in Philippa's life again—but hardly on the terms they had had before. This time he was cold and embittered, forcing her to agree to his terms and bent only on vengeance. What had happened to the love they had once shared? Could it be as easily dismissed as he seemed to think?

STARTING OVER

It was only eighteen months since Jo's life had collapsed in tragic circumstances, and she had still hardly reached the stage of picking up the pieces and making a fresh start. It was far too early, at any rate, to get involved with anyone as disturbing as Jake Marshall. Yet how could she avoid it?

TROPICAL KNIGHT

To pacify her mother, Ashleigh had agreed to pop up to Queensland for a few days to inspect her sister's new fiancé; she could, after all, just spare the time before she became immersed in plans for her own wedding to Jonathan. The new fiancé turned out to be more than satisfactory—which was more than Ashleigh could say for his disturbing cousin, Mitch Patrick. Thank goodness she wouldn't be seeing much more of *him*!

FORBIDDEN WINE

BY
LYNSEY STEVENS

MILLS & BOON LIMITED
15–16 BROOK'S MEWS
LONDON W1A 1DR

First published 1983
Australian copyright 1983
Philippine copyright 1983
This edition 1983

© Lynsey Stevens 1983

ISBN 0 263 74231 8

Set in Monophoto Times 11 on 11 pt.
01–0783 – 51179

Made and printed in Great Britain by
Richard Clay (*The Chaucer Press*) Ltd,
Bungay, Suffolk

For my Mum, with much love

CHAPTER ONE

BY turning her head a fraction Bree could bring the chiselled features of the man so close beside her in the confining aircraft seats into her peripheral vision, and that same awareness attacked her somewhere in the pit of her stomach. While his eyes were closed, long thick lashes for which a woman would have given her eye teeth, but darkly masculine for all that, resting on the tanned skin above his high cheekbones, she felt some safety in her illicit studying of him.

If he wasn't fully asleep at least he was dozing, lying back relaxed, and his hard features had softened somewhat. But he was still the most attractive man she had ever seen in her life. She was so very sure, excited sure, apprehensively sure, of that fact, even though this was the first time in the less than twenty-four hours she had known him that she had summoned enough nerve to give herself free reign to assimilate every last facet of his compelling masculinity.

Her eyes avidly took in each feature. His dark hair was swept tidily sideways, back from his face, flashes of distinguishing grey-white at the temples, and long enough to touch on his collar at the back. His forehead was wide and only faintly lined and his brows were darkly defined, arching above eyes she knew were the most incredibly vivid shade of blue she had seen, as blue as the sun-kissed Pacific Ocean she had skirted on her drive south to Sydney. His nose was straight and the deep creases on either side of his mouth accentuated the squareness of his determined jaw. That this steel was also apparent in his personality she had already learnt. No one stood in his way.

She had an almost overwhelming urge to reach out and run her fingers along the line of those furrows in his smooth cheeks, feel the beard-roughened texture of his skin, and her heartbeats skipped and then began to race. This was pure foolishness and so out of keeping with her character, and she chastised herself severely.

However, this self-beration had little effect on her eyes as, with a will of their own, they touched on the curve of his lips. Firm and straight, his bottom lip fuller than the top, promising a sensuality that was not contradicted in one line of the remainder of his body, his mouth seemed so blatantly masculine that Bree had a startling, outrageous desire to feel the hard pressure of it moving on the softness of her own. She bit her lip to still its tremble.

This thought disturbed her so much that it was some time before she felt the flush that had invaded her cheeks subside and she could marshall the remnants of her courage to look at him again.

He was over six feet tall, towered over her—and she was far from short, at five feet six—and he was broad-shouldered, his expensive tailored three-piece suit not disguising the bulge of muscle in his shoulders and arms, the breadth of his chest, his flat stomach and narrow hips. No businessman gone to fat, this one. He obviously kept himself very much in trim. She knew now that he was thirty-seven, but he possessed the sort of rugged good looks and basic bone structure that defied the conventional means of age assessment.

Relaxed back in his seat, his long legs were thrust out in front of him, his knees resting against the back of the seat in front of him and the dark material of his suit trousers stretched tautly across the muscles of his thighs.

Bree swallowed nervously at her daring and her eyes moved upwards again. He stirred at that moment and she started guiltily, her gaze swinging away to the fluffy cottonwool clouds massed below the window of the airbus. The glass threw back her own reflection, her pale face with its small nose and firm pointed chin, over-large smoky grey eyes, her lashes and brows dark compared to the silky fairness of her hair. This was long, reaching halfway down her back, and it fell in a shimmering curtain, straight except for one wave where it came away from its parting to one side of her forehead.

Her sudden movement disturbed the child in her arms, and he stretched his sturdy legs and waved his small fists as he settled back against her, his little body warm and soft. Bree looked down at him, searching for some resemblance to the man beside her in his baby features, but she could find none. Ben was simply himself, although his colouring was her own.

Even now she could scarcely believe the so radical changes that the past three short weeks had wrought in her life, and if it hadn't been for the tangible feel of the child in her arms she would have suspected she was hallucinating, that it was all some crazy inexplicable dream. Her eyes went back to the baby in dismay and the same loving urge to protect him, make it up to him for so many things, washed over her again, this beautiful child that was so innocently part of the man beside her and part of herself.

God knew, Ben hadn't asked to be born. But he had been born, and at seven months old he was all a healthy baby should be, despite his lack of care. Bree squeezed her eyes tightly closed, unwilling to allow herself to imagine the extent of Ben's neglect in the past few months. Oh, he'd been fed, but Bree rather suspected that was more to keep him quiet.

How could they do it to such a small defenceless baby? she asked herself once again. How could two people, supposedly old enough to conceive a child, simply shirk their responsibility for him? It was unforgivable.

Her thoughts went back three weeks and she remembered again receiving the letter that had seemed so opportune but which had set off the chain reaction of unbelievable coincidences that had brought her to the present moment, in an aircraft, with the baby and this magnetic man.

The letter was waiting for her at the dilapidated old house she shared with three other girls. She remembered how the bad luck that seemed to be dogging her had heightened her awareness, so that her eyes slid away in disgust from the peeling faded paint on the verandah and door as she went inside, going straight to her room. Setting her shoulderbag down on the small chest of drawers, she sank tiredly on to the ancient single bed and closed her eyes, trying to escape the room's dingy ugliness.

What was she to do? she asked herself for the hundredth time. Everything seemed to be happening at once. And it was all bad. How she'd managed to get through last night and today with at least an outward composure she would never know. Inside she was anything but calm. Her stomach churned and she had been unable to face any food. If she got any thinner she would be just bones and skin.

How was she going to manage without her job? There was a recession in the trade, said the foreman at the factory where she had worked for the past three months, since her return to Bundaberg, a town where she had spent part of her childhood. She had hated the boring repetitive work of the factory, but at least it had been work. Now they were afraid they would have to let her go, part of an economy measure to stave off a shutdown. She wasn't alone, for a dozen others had been retrenched as well. Which meant a dozen others now looking for jobs in an area where work was far from plentiful. Bundaberg was sugar and fluctuated with world sugar prices.

And on top of losing her job it seemed she had lost a place to live. When she had arrived home last night her flatmates had told her they had all decided to give up the house. They were moving into a larger place, with their boy-friends. It would be cheaper and closer to the township.

Of course, Bree could come, too. That is, if she was prepared to be paired off with Jane's boy-friend's brother. He was a nice guy, they told her, was real cute, had his own car and fancied Bree. Remember, she'd met him at the party last week? Bree cringed inside. Oh yes, she remembered all right—the pawing hands and wet mouth. She shuddered, knowing she couldn't even consider such a situation, couldn't contemplate sharing her body with someone she barely knew. Not even for a place to stay. She'd rather sleep in her car.

So here she was with no job after Friday and nowhere to live. She couldn't hope to pay the rent

on this house on her own and she knew her
meagre savings would never stretch to paying a
bond on another cheaper flat. Maybe she could
find some other girls to share?

Her eyes went around the depressing greyness of
the room, settling on the chest of drawers and the
lopsided wardrobe that contained her small amount
of clothes and all her worldly possessions. Not
much to show for eighteen, going on nineteen years,
she thought sadly. Some clothes, a few books, a
battered guitar and an ancient clapped-out Mini.
Bree Ransome, huge success! she jeered, and dashed
away the teardrops that gathered on her lashes.

Self-pitying tears wouldn't help, she sighed
despondently. She'd have a bath before the others
arrived home and then make herself a cup of tea.
Things would look brighter then, she told herself
without much conviction.

She stood up resolutely. Only then did she see
the white envelope on the rickety table by the bed.
Recognising the almost childish scrawl as Briony's,
she snatched it up and tore the letter open. Jane
must have put it in here this afternoon before she
left on her evening shift. And she had almost
missed it, had sat beside it for ages.

The letter was written in an even more
haphazard hand than usual, and Bree strained to
decipher the words her sister had written when in
what had obviously been an agitated state. As she
began to understand the gist of her sister's plea for
help she sank slowly back on to the bed.

The three months since Bree had left them had
been pure hell, Briony wrote. She couldn't cope
any more with anything. She was always fighting
with Reece and he'd threatened to leave her. She'd
even slapped the baby, and she was terrified she'd

do even worse. Could Bree please come back and
help her. She feared she was going insane.

There were more entreaties to write and let them
know as soon as possible if she could come. And
there was a postscript. Max Turner had gone;
Reece had kicked him out as he hadn't been
paying his share of the rent. So there was nothing
to stop Bree from coming back.

Bree re-read the letter and her heart constricted.
One of the reasons she had left Briony and Reece
had been to make them stand on their own feet
where the baby was concerned. They had both
been prepared to simply go on as though he didn't
exist, leaving him solely to Bree. Max Turner's
unwanted attentions had only precipitated her
decision to go. She wouldn't go back. Briony had
to learn to face her responsibilities.

But what about Ben? And her heart lurched
painfully as she thought of the things she had seen
on TV and read about child abuse. Could she just
ignore Briony's letter, sit back and do nothing for
the child she had cared for from the moment he
had been born? Could she do that to the only
family she had in the world? Leaving them, Briony
and Ben, over three months ago had been an
agonising wrench. But the situation had become
intolerable and she had had to make the break.

She looked down at the letter and sighed, recalling the feel of Ben's warm body, smelling of baby
powder, cradled in her arms, and she knew she
would have to go to them. Besides, there was nothing
to keep her here now. No job. No place to live.

So she had set out in her Mini, praying it would
last out the fourteen-hundred-kilometre journey
south to Sydney, and she would have made it on
Tuesday morning as she had told Briony she

would had it not been for a burst radiator hose. Luckily she was within a short walking distance of the outskirts of a township, but by the time she had found a phone box and called a mechanic she had been held up for hours.

It was almost three o'clock before she turned into the narrow suburban Sydney street where Reece and Briony rented a far from new flat. As she pulled her suitcase and guitar out of the car she stopped and looked up at more peeling paintwork and sighed dejectedly. Somehow the block of flats looked even more run down than it had when she had left it only months ago.

Averting her gaze, she began the climb up the three flights of stairs, and wrinkled her nose in distaste as the familiar odour of stale cooking smells, musty dampness and uncleanliness rose up to meet her. She stumbled over the last step and her suitcase clattered to the bare dusty floor, the sound echoing down the dimly lit hallway that completely missed the touch of sunlight. Reece and Briony's flat was down the end of the passage. When a door opposite her opened she started in fright.

'About time you came back, too,' growled the woman of indeterminable age, her bright red hair adorned with curlers bobbing disapprovingly. 'That's kid's been crying all day, seems like. You've got no right to put us through it, having to listen to it squawling for hours on end. You take it from me, girlie, you and that young layabout you're living with, next time I'll have the Services on you, you see if I don't! Coming and going at all hours!'

The door slammed before Bree could reply or even begin to understand what the woman meant. She juggled her case and guitar along the narrow passage. Obviously the woman had mistaken her for Briony. It wasn't the first time. They could have passed for twins, although Bree's long silky hair was a shade or two fairer than her younger sister's.

Reaching the door, she tiredly set down her suitcase and knocked. There wasn't a sound from within and she knocked again, louder this time. No one answered, and Bree could have sank down on the floor and cried. They must have gone out. But surely, knowing she was coming, they could have left a note. Her hand reached for the door knob and it turned easily, the door swinging inwards.

'Briony? Reece?' She stepped tentatively inside.

The furniture was as she remembered it, the discoloured and sagging sofa, the two vinyl-covered armchairs, their colours mismatched and clashing, and the dark threadbare carpet. The small kitchenette and dining table were off to one side and the doors to both small bedrooms were standing open. As Bree stood there undecided a sound came from the room she had used when she had lived here.

'Briony?' She called again, louder, her voice echoing in the emptiness, and the sound came again, a soft hiccuping cry.

Bree was across the room in a flash, her case and guitar dropping to the floor. The small bed was unmade and the faded curtains stirred as an indifferent breeze squeezed in through the partly open window. Her eyes growing accustomed to the dimness, she swung her gaze aside to the cot, her legs heavy as she moved towards it, her throat closing on the cry that rose inside her as she looked down on her nephew.

At first she feared the worst, he lay there so still, but as she fought for breath he moved a tiny fist and gave that same hoarse cry, his eyelids, red and swollen from crying, fluttering open.

'Oh, Ben! Ben!' Bree choked as tears of relief and pain coursed down her cheeks. She reached into the cot and gathered him into her arms, the sight of him in such a state of distress making her legs go weak beneath her. She cradled him to her, crooning softly to him, her heart a cold heavy ache in her chest. How could . . .?

But there was no time for questions when there was no one here to answer them. The baby was soaked through, so she set about changing him, sponging him down, finding and applying a soothing cream to his raw skin, heating his bottle and feeding him slowly, holding him until he had fallen asleep. Reluctantly she tucked him into the single bed, propping pillows around him as an improvised cot as his own bed was still wet, and she stood gazing down at him, the pain in her heart searing through her.

How could his own mother leave him in such a state? Surely Briony wouldn't have done it on purpose? Maybe they'd had an accident, or . . .? But they still must have left him here in the flat alone, and that was unforgivable.

Tension ached behind her eyes and her fingers gently massaged her temples as she walked slowly back into the living-room. Perhaps a cup of tea would help. She moved towards the small stove to reheat the kettle. Only then did she see the note propped up on the wall unit. She must have been too engrossed in bathing and feeding the baby to have noticed it before.

Her eyes skimmed her sister's writing and the

piece of paper fell to the floor from her nerveless fingers. No—it couldn't be! She must be dreaming. Briony wouldn't . . . . She couldn't believe it of her own sister. Briony couldn't have written the note. Surely, as the baby's mother, she . . .

But then again, Briony had never wanted Ben, would have had an abortion if she, Bree, hadn't talked her out of it. Her teeth began to chatter and she slowly retrieved the note and sank down in the armchair, her eyes seeking out her sister's words like a tongue-tip probing a sensitive tooth.

'Dear Bree,' she re-read, 'I'm sorry to dump all this in your lap, but you were the only one I could turn to, and knowing how you feel about Ben, I knew you'd hate it if I'd left him to anyone else. Please don't judge me too harshly, you know I never wanted a child, and understand that Reece is everything to me. Things have been going wrong between us ever since I found out I was pregnant, and having the baby only made it worse. This grotty flat, motherhood and playing house just isn't for me. I tried, Bree—I really did. But it didn't work.

'Now Reece has the offer of a job with a new band that's forming up. You know what a fantastic guitarist he is, and the group is really keen to have him. After a few engagements in the country areas they have offers of plenty of work on the islands up north. It's his big chance. That's no life for a baby and I know neither of us could cope with it.

'I know you care about the baby more than I ever could. He'd have been better off with you as his mother anyway. Please don't hate me for this but Reece would have gone without me. I won't say look after Ben because I know you will. Briony.'

Bree leant back against the seat and closed her eyes, all of a sudden her aching muscles reminding her of her days at the wheel of her car, and she realised her whole body was throbbing painfully. She glanced at her wrist watch, surprised to see that she'd been at the flat for over two hours, two hours since she had unsuspectingly pulled up outside the block of flats, prepared to be reunited with her sister.

She stood up stiffly and walked quietly back into the bedroom to check on the baby, her eyes filling with tears as she looked down at him, recalling the moment she had found him, alone, hungry and wet, totally exhausted with crying, his little face red and damp. Who could say how long he had been left there, for Briony and Reece could have deserted him hours earlier. What if she hadn't arrived today? She shuddered at the thought.

Sinking down on the end of the bed, she pulled a rough blanket over her as tiredness and the after-effects of the shock of finding Ben here alone caught up with her and she fell into a deep sleep beside the baby, not stirring until he did the next morning.

The days flew by, days that were completely filled, not giving her time for soul-searching thought. Looking after the baby and searching desperately and futilely for a job left her physically exhausted by nightfall and she knew she had grown impossibly thinner. Most of her savings had gone on the rent, paying the month Reece and Briony had been in arrears as well as the current month, and in less that two weeks' time she would have to find the money for another month's payment.

Yesterday she had been forced to pawn her

guitar, and this afternoon she had sold her car. Given it away, she grimaced. The car dealer had gone to great lengths to point out the Mini's faults and defects, and she knew he hadn't given her nearly what it was worth. But she'd needed the money to keep them going until she could collect her unemployment benefits or found work of some kind that would fit in with looking after Ben. Any job was hard to come by, let alone one that would enable her to manage a small baby.

At first she had expected to hear from Briony, but as the days passed she began to realise that her sister had no intention of returning or keeping in touch. Briony had severed her ties.

Her consolation was that Ben was thriving. His thin little body had begun to fill out and his bright eyes, the exact shade of hers and Briony's, followed her trustingly, his grin showing four small perfect teeth, filling her with a love that hurt. Before there had only been Briony, a younger sister to be loved and protected. But Briony had flung off such bonds quite early, letting Bree know she had no intention of being answerable to anyone, not even her sister. Briony had always gone her own way. The baby was different. He depended on her and accepted her loving attention without reservation.

The love she felt for Ben was also ravelled up with an ever-present guilt, guilt that whatever befell Ben was somehow her responsibility, for had she not stopped her sister then Briony would have terminated her pregnancy and Ben would never have been born. And Bree knew she had been against the abortion for all the wrong reasons.

She had no all-consuming feelings for or against abortion itself. And she hadn't asked herself if

Briony was ready for motherhood, if Reece had been prepared to accept the responsibility for his child. She'd only seen the baby in terms of a family, part of the real flesh-and-blood family that she and Briony had never had. Her own father she couldn't remember and her mother was only a faint recollection, for she had been barely five years old and Briony four when they had been put in the care of the State Children's Services. The remainder of their childhood had been spent in various foster-homes until Bree had been old enough to earn her own living.

She only knew that she couldn't let Briony give up her child, and amazingly Briony had listened to her, deciding to have Ben and keep him, even though Reece seemed indifferent to her decision. Now, looking back on the situation as objectively as she could, Bree knew she had been wrong to try to make her sister, then sixteen, feel an emotion she obviously didn't feel, experience something with which she was far too young, too immature, to cope. As she settled Ben in his cot she gently ran her hand over his soft fair hair and silently promised to do her best for him.

Later in the evening she was sitting mending a pair of her faded old jeans, keeping the worrying thoughts about money as far from her mind as possible, when the knock came on the door of the flat. Had it only been the night before last? she asked herself incredulously as the plane flew over the New South Wales coast on its journey northwards. Somehow, that frightful night seemed to be part of some other life, some other time.

It was reasonably early, perhaps eightish, when the knock made her start with fright, but she sprang up nevertheless, her first thoughts of

Briony. Of course she realised now that she had been foolish to fling open the door without asking who was outside, but she hadn't even thought past her sister.

He was inside the flat before she had the chance to slam the door in his face and he reached out and pushed the door closed behind him, his eyes, small and beady in his face, peering at her with cruel amusement. Her blood ran cold at the sight of him. He was the last person she expected to see, the last person she wanted to see.

'Well, doll. How goes the frigid little Brigit?' he smirked at his own cleverness and a shiver of real fear crept up her spine.

Max Turner had been a friend of Reece's, although the only thing they seemed to have in common was the fact that they both rode motor-bikes, for Max was a good three or four years older than Reece. Reece at least had been reasonably clean; Max Turner always looked grimy. To-night he appeared even more dirty and uncouth.

He had the rough-textured skin, lank non-descript hair and off-colour teeth that didn't help his appearance, and Bree had always found him repulsive. When he had been evicted from his lodgings Reece had let him sleep on the sofa until he found a new place, but Max had come and stayed. Even Briony had disliked him.

His eyes always seemed to rest on Bree, his leer mentally undressing her, making her skin crawl, and his suggestive innuendoes and persistent pawing had been the final straw in her decision to leave. In the end he had taken to pulling her into his arms when they were alone, finding her rebuffing gestures, her pleas for him to leave her alone a come-on. Her appeal to Reece to speak to

Max had been to no avail. Reece was belligerent and out of sorts with Briony, so he wasn't prepared to do anything for her sister. She knew she had to leave, before Max's passes became serious, and not the cruel game they had been up till then.

Now he stood in front of her, his eyes roaming over the agitated rise and fall of her breasts in her loose cotton shirt, dropping lower to the long length of her legs in jeans that were a little baggy from her loss of weight.

If anything he revolted her even more. His own jeans were grease-ingrained, tucked into long leather motorcycle boots that were dusty and stained, and over his grubby T-shirt he wore a padded leather sleeveless battle jacket. He needed a shave, and as he wiped his matted hair back from his face she saw the grease under his fingernails and on his hands.

'Lost your tongue, Miss Toffee-Nose?' he asked as he dropped his crash helmet on the floor and walked towards her.

Bree took a couple of steps backwards until her legs came up against the sofa. She couldn't stop herself moving away from him.

'Not very sociable, are you? How about a beer? I'm parched.' He was a mere foot away from her.

'I . . . There's no beer,' she got out.

He gave a harsh laugh and she smelled the stale alcohol and nicotine on his breath. 'That figures!' he said contemptuously. 'You wouldn't want to lower the class of this magnificent apartment.'

'I . . . Reece . . .' She did a double take, realising just how physically isolated she was. If he thought she was alone—Oh, God! 'Reece isn't home yet,' she said, her voice high with her fear.

Laughing, Max threw himself aside into one of the armchairs. 'Reece isn't home yet,' he mocked, as she measured the distance to the door. Even if she made it outside who could she call for assistance? The other tenants wouldn't want to know.

'And he won't be home, so you can cut the crap,' Max sneered at her.

'What do you mean?' she tried to brazen it out.

'I mean I know as well as you do that he's gone. With your sister. They've left. Cleared off.'

Bree could only watch him, the fear now even more real, rising until it seemed to spout through the pores of her skin. His eyes were all over her again. God, if he touched her she'd die! He pushed himself upright and her eyes widened, every muscle tensing.

'So! There's just you and me.' He laughed again. 'Me and you.' His finger came out to touch the button of her shirt where it rested between her breasts.

In panic Bree made a dash for the safety of the bedroom, but he grabbed her long hair, pulled her viciously backwards until his hand fastened on her arm and he dragged her back to the sofa, not caring that she cried out in pain.

'Don't be like that, Bree. You should be nice to me. You owe me.'

'Owe you?' she got out, her hands trying to pull his away from her arm.

'Sure. For all the sleep I lost while you wriggled that little backside of yours in front of me and then fobbed me off with your nose in the air, always thinking you were too good for me. I haven't forgotten that,' he growled.

'I didn't . . .' she began, her voice cracking as she strained away from him.

'Shut up, you teasing little bitch!' he snarled. 'No, I haven't forgotten. I've waited a long time for this and I'm sure going to enjoy it.' His lips came down and Bree turned her head away, only to have his fingers twist painfully in her hair to pull her mouth back so that his could cover her lips.

With his weight leaning over her and her legs against the chair, she overbalanced, falling on her back on the sofa, Max's body on top of her knocking the breath out of her. His lips ground against her teeth and she groaned in pain, tasting her own blood. His hands fumbled for her breasts and the thin cotton of her shirt tore loudly, the sound seeming to explode in the room, galvanising her into action.

She fought him with every breath, every ounce of strength in her body, her fingernails scratching at him as she heard her sobs, her cries for help, from some way off from herself. He put his hand over her mouth to stifle her screams, swearing at her, using words she barely knew existed, and her teeth clamped down on the flesh of his hand even as the bile rose in her throat to choke her.

'You little bitch! I'll teach you to bite me!' he yelled, and his hand went up to strike her.

Bree closed her eyes, tensing, waiting for the blow. But it never came.

Instead Max's weight was suddenly wrenched off her and the coldness left behind him seemed to burn her bare breasts. She lay quite still, her eyes closed, holding her breath, not daring to believe it had stopped.

CHAPTER TWO

THE sound of Max's body hitting the floor had her eyes flying open in time to see him sprawled his length, blood pouring from his nose as he moaned faintly. Her eyes flashed from his still form to the stranger turning menacingly from Max to face her. Terror momentarily returned and she drew a sharp calming breath, then fought for control, her eyes beginning to register his appearance.

From her low position on the sofa the stranger stood over her like some ancient colossus, and in those few seconds she had an indelible impression of height, of breadth of muscular shoulders, of dark hair flashing silver-white at the temples, a rugged compelling face and the very bluest eyes she had ever seen.

Those eyes left Max's prostrate figure, went steadily to meet her gaze and then fell to her torn shirt, the bareness of her breasts. Bree sat up in agitation, covering herself with her hands, her face paling. Her head spun and she felt the nausea rise within her. She lunged for the bathroom, scarcely reaching the basin in time before she was horribly sick.

She sank weakly on to the tiled floor, her body aching, her throat raw. Then firm hands had pulled her upright and a cool wet towel was being wiped over her face, taking her tangled hair back from her forehead.

'Sit there for a moment,' he said, and pushed

her on to the toilet seat. 'If you feel faint put your head down between your knees.'

He left her then and she closed her eyes, gulping deep breaths of air. She wiped her face again and gingerly stood up, pulling off the tatters of her shirt, shuddering as the telltale bruises began to appear on her breasts. Her short towelling bathrobe was hanging behind the door and she shrugged it on, tying the cord tightly about her. Taking another steadying breath she went slowly back into the living-room.

Max had gone and the stranger was spooning tea leaves into the teapot. Bree walked across towards the kitchen and he looked up, his eyes piercing her for a few seconds before he turned to set the mugs on the counter top. She had no doubt that in those few infinite moments he had taken in every inch of her.

'I . . . Where's Max?' she asked, her voice thick and rawly husky.

'Max? Is that his name?' His voice was like the deep liquid tones of a throbbing piece of music. 'I discouraged him from wanting to stay,' he said simply, and Bree shivered at the sudden steel in the hard length of his body.

The silence echoed and she ventured a few steps closer to him.

'Thank you,' she faltered, feeling herself blush, 'for what you did. I don't think I could have kept fighting for much longer.'

'I take it you did want me to intervene?' he asked evenly, casually pouring boiling water into the teapot.

'Yes!' The word burst out of her and she began to shake uncontrollably.

He came around the wall unit then and his arms

went around her, one hand holding her head against his chest. She could hear his heart beating, a strong steady thudding, and she relaxed a little, the shaking subsiding as she savoured the safety of the strength he exuded. Of their own accord her arms slipped naturally around his waist.

She felt him tense and thought his heartbeats quickened, but it was only momentary and she might have imagined it, for by then the male odour of him, a cleanness, a faint tinge of musky aftershave lotion, was in her nostrils and she caught her breath sharply, feeling a whole new sensation beginning to tease the pit of her stomach, rising to spread through her entire body. She was just as suddenly aware of the impression of her breasts against the wall of his chest and her own heartbeats began to echo in her head.

'Who was he?'

She felt his voice vibrate through her and her skin tingled in waves of pleasure.

'Max. His name's Max Turner. He's a friend of Reece's. He ...' She shuddered again and he stepped away to look down at her through narrowed lids. Regretfully she let her hands fall from his waist. 'Just the thought of him touching me makes me sick to my stomach,' she said quietly, and he raised a dark eyebrow, the creases in his cheeks deepening wryly.

'That I believe,' he said, and turned back to reach for the teapot. 'Come and drink this.'

She followed him and slid on to a chair at the small table. He took the chair opposite her, the solidness of him dwarfing the kitchenette. Bree sipped her tea thankfully, feeling it reach down to warm her bruised stomach, although she winced as the heat stung her cut mouth.

'Thank you for this, too,' she said, motioning to the cup of tea.

He shrugged and raised his own mug to his lips.

'I haven't asked you how you came to be here?' she asked, trying to piece together the sequence of events. The knock on the door. Max bursting in, pushing the door after she'd tried to slam it in his face. Max mustn't have closed the door properly. Thank God! she shivered. 'It was lucky for me that you were passing, Mr ...' she looked at him enquiringly.

He didn't answer her immediately, but his blue eyes watched her steadily. They were incredible eyes, held you enmeshed in their fathomless depths.

'Durant,' he said at last. 'Heath Durant.'

'Thank you, Mr Durant.' She managed a smile as he continued to watch her carefully, seeming to gauge her reaction, and she shifted uneasily in her seat.

'The name doesn't mean anything to you?' he asked, his eyes not leaving her face.

She regarded him questioningly. 'No. No, I don't think so.' She frowned. 'Should it?'

His eyes then went to the mug enveloped in his hand. 'Obviously not. You mentioned a Reece a moment ago?' His eyes impaled her again.

'Yes. Reece Andrews. He ...' She paused momentarily. 'He used to live here,' she finished quietly.

'Andrews.' He grimaced and said something she couldn't catch under his breath.

'Do you know Reece?' she asked, and it occurred to her that perhaps Reece owed this man money.

Heath Durant reached inside his coat pocket

and drew out a photograph. 'Is that him?' he asked expressionlessly.

'Why, yes. Yes, it is. You do know him, then?' She looked at him in surprise. A debt collector would hardly be carrying a photograph of Reece around with him.

'You could say that,' he replied dryly and returned the photo to his pocket. 'Have you,' there was an infinitesimal pause, 'known Reese long?'

Something in his tone brought a touch of colour to her cheeks. Surely he didn't think that she and Reece . . .? 'I've known him for about eighteen months. We . . . We all met in Bundaberg. He was playing in a band there.'

His lips tightened. 'And where is he now?'

Bree looked down at the table. 'I don't know. He's just joined another group. I'm not sure where they were going.'

Those blue eyes were on her again, as though he was looking into her very soul.

'And where are your parents?' he asked, his eyes leaving her to move around the shabbiness of the flat. 'Do they know where you're living?'

'I haven't any parents,' she said flatly.

'Haven't any, or have you simply cut yourself off from them?' His face held a cold cyncism.

'It's the truth. I have no parents,' she told him with a flash of anger. 'Why would I say I had no parents if I did?'

Before he could comment Ben gave a loud cry, demanding attention, and Bree stood up, pausing at the expression on Heath Durant's face. He looked as though he had been struck. His face had tensed and his lips thinned as his eyes raked her too slender body.

She turned and almost bolted from the room,

not understanding the emotions in that expression, or the currents that emanated from him. Strangely he thrilled and yet terrified her.

Ben's cry became a gurgle of laughter as she bent over him. Deftly she changed his wet nappy and tickled him under the chin.

'You should be asleep, young man,' she laughed with him. 'Now I don't suppose you'll want to close those bright eyes and go back to sleep, will you?'

He laughed and reached his arms out for her and she lifted him up, planting a quick kiss on the tip of his nose. She turned to pick up the light rug to wrap around him, stopping as she caught sight of a tall figure leaning in the bedroom doorway. Her eyes slid away from him, her face colouring, as she gently wrapped the baby in his rug.

'This is Ben,' she said, when the silence stretched between them.

The stranger's eyes went from her face to the baby, who met his gaze with interest, one finger shoved in his mouth.

'He looks like you,' Heath Durant said softly.

'He has the same colouring as I do,' she said carefully. 'He's fair like . . . like me,' she finished, loath to go into the story. Let him think what he cared to think!

'Where's his father?' he asked bluntly, and Bree's blush deepened.

What could she say? From his tone he thought he'd summed up the situation.

'Or should I say, who's his father?'

'Does that matter?' She played for time.

He shrugged. 'It should to you.' His tone was indifferent. 'It might to him one day,' he added cruelly, an edge to his voice.

Bree tensed with anger, her arms tightening around the baby and he murmured protestingly. 'Perhaps it will.' She strove for dignity. 'It's Reece—Reece Andrews,' she told him, only as soon as the words were spoken she regretted them, not fully understanding why she'd said what she did. What did she care what he thought? She didn't have to answer to him, whoever he was. She knew he thought Ben was hers. And yet she didn't want him thinking she was capable of the sordid affairs his cynical expression was implying.

He stood slowly away from the door jamb, his whole stance now one of tense controlled volatile violence. The brilliant blue eyes were sabre thrusts that ran through her and she stepped backwards, holding Ben away from him, knowing an urge to protect him with her body.

'Is that the truth?' he ground out.

'Of course. Why ... why would I lie about that?' she answered breathlessly.

'Why indeed. Can you prove it?'

'Prove it? I don't see why I should have to prove it to you.'

He reached her in two strides. 'I said, can you prove it?' he repeated, his hand clamping on her arm.

Bree stared up at him with wide frightened eyes, as his anger enveloped her. 'Yes. His birth certificate—I have that. It's in the drawer over there.'

'Get it!' he demanded.

'I really don't see why ...' she began.

'Get it!' His tone was deathly quiet, but he let go of her arm.

Holding Ben close to her, she walked over to the dressing table, sliding open the top drawer and leafing through the few papers inside. 'Here it is.' She turned back to him and he was right behind her.

He opened out the certificate, his eyes reading quickly. Glancing up at her, he began to read it aloud. 'Benjamin Reece. Father, Reece Andrews. Mother, Briony Maree Ransome. There's no indication of a marriage,' he remarked, and her eyes fell. 'Why not?' She remained silent and his finger lifted her chin. 'Why not?'

'Reece said ... he didn't believe in marriages, that they were just pieces of paper.'

His lips thinned. 'Of course—Reece would. Anything to knock his idea of the establishment,' he said with quiet bitterness, and then seemed to gather himself together. 'Pack your things,' he ordered uncompromisingly.

Bree stared at him. 'What are you talking about?'

'I'm talking about your clothes, yours and the baby's. Pack them, Briony Ransome.'

'It's Bree Ransome,' she said automatically.

'Briony—Bree. Whatever. Pack your things.' He turned and lifted her suitcase down from the top of the wardrobe. 'You're coming with me.'

'You're mad! I don't even know you. Just because you—well, you helped me out before it doesn't mean you can order me about. Why should I come with you?' Her breath quickened.

'If you want to stay with the child you'll come.' He threw the suitcase on to the bed and opened the door of the wardrobe, grabbing her small amount of clothes in one armful and flinging them into the case.

'If I want ...?' Fear gripped her. 'What do you mean by that?' she all but yelled at him, and Ben whimpered at the tone of her voice.

'I mean, Miss Ransome, that no grandson of mine is going to stay in this flea infested rat-hole.'

'Grandson! Grandson?' Her voice cracked incredulously and she knew an hysterical urge to laugh. The man standing in front of her was so far removed from her preconceptions of a grandfather figure that it was ridiculously funny. 'You can't be serious!' she spluttered.

'I can't?' His voice was so dangerously quiet that she sobered.

'I mean, you'd have to be Reece's father to be . . .' Her words faded away and he raised one dark eyebrow. Bree stared at him open-mouthed. 'You don't look old enough to be Reece's father.'

He gave a short bitter laugh. 'I'm thirty-seven. Reece is eighteen.'

'Your name's Durant. You said it was and . . . you're Reece's father?' she finished quietly.

'I have that,' he paused slightly, 'dubious honour.'

'But how could you be?'

He gave a humourless laugh. 'I'm sure I don't need to explain to you the mechanics of that,' he said drily, looking pointedly at Ben, and she flushed hotly.

This was the moment to tell him she wasn't Ben's mother, but something held her back, made her cautious.

'Reece never mentioned that he had a family,' she said warily.

'He wouldn't. Reece and I didn't see eye to eye on many things. On most things. So he decided to go his own way, without telling anyone about his intentions. It's taken me eighteen months to track him down.'

'You've been looking for him all that time?'

He inclined his head. 'I've been looking for him all that time. He's been on the Missing Persons List at the Police Department for the best part of a year.'

Bree couldn't take it in. Never once had Reece even hinted that he had parents living. 'How did you find him?' she asked.

'A stroke of luck really. I was here on business and I heard second-hand that there was a new band forming up and that the guitarist was called Reece. It's not a common name, so it was worth a chance. I was given this address.'

'It was lucky for me,' she agreed softly.

Heath Durant glanced down at his gold wristwatch. 'It's getting late. We'd better get a move on.'

'I can't go with you,' Bree began. 'I mean, I'm sorry, but I don't know you and—well, I can't leave the flat.'

Those piercing eyes watched her steadily, speculatively, and she looked away, holding Ben closer as his head dropped sleepily on to her shoulder.

'Can't or won't?' he asked quietly.

Bree swallowed nervously, not knowing how to answer him.

'Is Reece coming back?'

She looked up at him then and shook her head. 'No.'

'But you feel there's always a chance that if you wait here he might,' he suggested flatly.

'No. There's no chance he'll come back. I told you, he's gone with the band somewhere in the country.'

'Then there's nothing to stop you coming with me. You've no parents, no job, I take it?' he queried, and she shook her head. 'As I said, there's nothing to keep you here.'

Nothing, she silently agreed with him. Nothing but the trepidation of the new feelings he generated within her. They were sensations she'd never experienced before, and she fought down the hunger that urged her not to sever the connection with him. Her whole body cried out to know more of him, and she felt the telltale blush flood her cheeks.

'I can't expect you to take the responsibility for us,' she started breathlessly.

'I'm not doing it because it's expected of me,' he said with a frown of irritation. 'The child's part of my family.'

'Not legally,' she averted her eyes.

'Morally,' he stated.

'But I haven't got much money at the moment and I can't pay our way. I . . .'

'If you haven't got a job or money how do you expect to exist? How did Reece expect you to manage?' He stood facing her, hands agressively on his hips.

'The rent's paid for the next few weeks. By then I'll . . . I'll have a job . . .'

'What sort of job do you think you'll get with the child to look after?' he rapped out.

'Well, I . . .'

He gave an exclamation of disgust and turned away from her for a moment. His hands were still on his hips and his jacket stretched tautly over the width of his muscular back. As he turned suddenly back to face her his eyes ran over the length of her, her old jeans and the faded bathrobe, and he said something under his breath.

'For heaven's sake, you look like you haven't

had a proper meal in months, and this place could hardly be called a palace,' he waved a hand to encompass the pokey little room.

'It's clean,' she said defensively. 'And I do eat when I'm hungry.' Except that lately there seemed to be so much to do, and cooking for herself was a huge effort.

'All right. It's clean and you eat, but what I say stands. I don't care to have my son's child brought up in this environment.'

'And doesn't a child's mother have any say?' Bree cried angrily, and their eyes locked together across the small space.

'Pack your things, Miss Ransome. I have no intention of leaving here without the boy. He goes—with or without you. And, unlike you, I do have money, so I can afford to do it all legally.' His face was set and his eyes were suddenly dark pools of gunmetal grey.

'You can't mean that you'd try to take Ben away from me? No court in the world would give Ben to you, take a child from its mother.' As she said the word a cold chill enveloped her heart. Mother—the operative word. She wasn't Ben's mother, so she hadn't a leg to stand on. This stranger with the will of steel held the trump card, whether he knew it or not. And if he started to delve around he'd . . .

'Would you want it dragged through the courts?' he broke quietly into her thoughts and her eyes flickered tiredly downwards. 'Come on, pack the child's things.' His voice was soft and persuasive but still held the note of command for all that. 'I'll get in touch with the landlord and leave a forwarding address with him in case Reece does come back here.'

'The landlord lives on the premises, in flat one,' she told him. 'But surely we could wait until tomorrow?' Her words established her capitulation.

He was watching her still, unsettling her. 'Tonight,' he said firmly. 'Finish packing and I'll speak to the landlord.' He turned and was gone, leaving the small dingy bedroom suddenly empty and indescribably lonely.

Her old suitcase and a couple of cardboard cartons easily held their things, hers and Ben's, and their shabbiness seemed to jeer at her as she sat in the uncomfortable armchair nursing the sleeping baby, waiting for Heath Durant to return. Her eyes went to the sofa and she shuddered as she recalled what might have happened if Max Turner hadn't been stopped. Rape was an ugly word, and she felt her stomach churn again.

In her adolescent dreams, when she had time to indulge in them, she saw herself in a long gossamer and lace dress with a screening veil, just like the pictures she saw in magazines. Waiting in the shadows was a tall dark man, his eyes alight with a love that was hers alone. And the wonder of giving herself for the first time to him was for Bree the most precious part of it all. And Max Turner had very nearly ruined that.

Perhaps she was old-fashioned, but that was how she felt. Quite often in the past she had been told she was frigid or worse, and even Briony had laughed at her when Bree had tried to talk her sister out of going to live with Reece.

'People don't think like you do any more. Thank God!' added Briony with feeling. 'Life's to be lived, Bree. You can't wait for it to happen. You may wait for ever. Not me—I take what I can when it's there to be taken. Men always have, so why not us?'

'But you're both so young,' Bree protested. 'What if you change your minds about each other in a year or so?'

'I won't. I know I won't. But if we do—well, so what? There'll be someone else.' Briony laughed at her sister's surprised expression. 'You don't think Reece is the first guy I've been to bed with, do you? Hell, Bree, where have you been all these years?'

Bree's face had paled. She hadn't once thought, once suspected that Briony . . .

'You mean you didn't know?' Briony looked at Bree as though she'd never seen her before. 'You didn't, I can see that.'

'Briony, it's not right. What if you got pregnant?'

'Nobody gets pregnant these days,' said Briony confidently. 'There is such a thing as the pill, you know!'

Bree flushed, feeling as if she in turn was seeing Briony for the first time, not as her younger sister but as a modern girl about town, and she didn't care for what she saw.

'You've never been to bed with a guy, have you?' Briony asked straight out, and Bree felt her face wash with colour.

'I happen to think that's my own business. It's private, not something you discuss like you would the weather or something,' she replied defensively, angry with herself for feeling she was in the wrong.

'You haven't!' Briony said blatantly. 'That's priceless! No wonder all the guys give you up for a dead loss! You take it from me, you'll never get a man if you keep that attitude, not in this day and age. And anyway, don't knock swimming if you've never been in the water yourself,' she smirked.

And where had Briony's attitude got her? Bree reflected ruefully. A weekend party, and somehow she'd forgotten to take her pill, and then there was Ben.

She looked down at the baby sleeping peacefully in her arms. Oh, Ben, she appealed to him, what should I do for the best? Should I cut and run now while I have the chance or go with this virtual stranger? What's best for you, that's the point?

'I do have money,' Heath Durant had said, and Bree believed him. He looked successful. It wasn't simply that his clothes were obviously expensive or that his shoes were of hand-tooled leather. Success seemed to emanate from every inch of him. He could do so much more for Ben than she could. She shivered as she brought her memory's image of him into her mind.

'I'll put these in the car and come back for the suitcase.' The sound of his voice made her start and she blinked up at him. 'I won't be long.' He set off with the two cartons and was back in no time at all.

Bree followed him out of the flat, her eyes sweeping the depressing room before she snapped off the light and closed the door, not finding an ounce of regret to be leaving it. And conversely there was no anticipation of their destination as she sank back in the plush seat of Heath Durant's Fairlane.

Now that they were mobile he seemed loath to talk, and as they drove through the darkened suburbs Bree tried to relax. Under cover of the dimly lit interior of the car she watched his hands on the steering wheel and found her heartbeats skipping erratically. He had good hands, strong and capable. She drew a steadying breath.

Reece's father—he couldn't be! They were as different as chalk and cheese. Reece could never come near this man in stature, in self-possession, in any way imaginable. Perhaps Reece took after his mother as Ben did.

Reece's mother. She'd never given her a thought. Bree swallowed quickly, feeling as though she'd been dealt a stunning blow. Reece's mother. Somehow the thought of a woman, for she would be nearing forty to have married this man, had his child . . . A chilling pain seemed to race through her and she bit her lip.

What a fool she'd been to nurture any slim shred of hope that someone as attractive, as successful as Heath Durrant would even notice her. She squeezed her eyes tightly closed in an effort to block out the painful pictures her mind conjured up of Heath Durant and his wife. And she had made the commitment to go with him to his home. Their home.

There must be some way to get out of this. Her eyes slid sideways. She would have to tell him she had changed her mind, that it was impossible. But at that moment they swung into an underground car park and drew to a halt in a space by the elevator.

'Where are we?' she asked breathily, her heart in her mouth, almost choking her.

'At my hotel.' He removed the keys from the ignition.

'Your hotel? But I thought . . .' Bree swallowed. 'I thought we were going to your home.'

'We are. Tomorrow,' he stated easily, and climbed out of the car, striding around to hold the passenger side door open for her.

Slowly Bree followed him into the elevator, stood with him in the sterile confines of it as it slid soundlessly upwards for what seemed like ages. His suite was luxurious in Bree's eyes, far grander than anything she had seen outside of magazines.

'You'd better settle the child.' He strode across and opened one of two doors off the sitting room. 'I had them bring a cot up for him.'

Bree stared at him open-mouthed.

'I phoned from the landlord's flat,' he explained, and set her suitcase on the low table at the end of the large double bed. 'The bathroom's through there.' He indicated the door. 'I'll be out in the sitting room when you've finished.'

When he left her Bree tucked Ben into the cot and he settled down, the drive not disturbing his sleep. Bree looked about her, running her hand over the polished surface of the bed end, feeling the satiny bedspread. The bathroom was a mass of pale blue tiles and shining chrome fittings. There was an identical door to the one she had used leading out of the opposite side of the bathroom, and she quietly turned the knob and peeped into another bedroom. It was much the same as her own and there was a brown leather suitcase, partly unpacked, with a dark blue jacket draped across it on the bed. Just as quietly she closed the door and walked back through her room and into the sitting room.

'Right.' Heath Durant had his back to her and was speaking into the telephone. 'Flight Two Fifteen at ten in the morning. Thanks.' He replaced the receiver and picked up the drink that sat beside the telephone. Downing the amber liquid in one gulp, he grimaced down at the empty glass and set it on the small coffee table. As he

turned slightly he caught sight of Bree standing
there.

'Would you like something to drink?' he asked.

'No, thanks.' She stood uncertainly, her hands
clasped in front of her as she searched for
something to say to him.

'Sit down.' He motioned a little shortly to a soft
armchair and she subsided into it as he took the
chair opposite her.

'Do you live far out of Sydney?' Bree asked him
nervously.

A crooked smile briefly touched his lips. 'About
eleven hundred kilometres.'

'Eleven hundred . . .' Bree sat up with a start.
'But you said we were going there tomorrow!'

'We are. I've just booked our seats on a flight in
the morning,' he told her calmly.

'Flight?' she repeated parrot-fashion.

'Flight. To Brisbane.'

Bree opened her mouth and closed it again.
'You didn't say anything about going to Brisbane.
I thought—in fact, you let me think you lived here
in Sydney.'

'I did?' He raised his dark eyebrow. 'I
mentioned that I was here on business, which I
am. That's all.'

'But this is ridiculous! I can't go flying to
Brisbane.'

'Why not? Don't you like Brisbane and the
Sunshine State?'

'Of course I like it, what I've seen of it, but . . .'

'But . . .?' he repeated with infuriating calmness.

'Look, how do I know you're Reece's father? I
only have your word for it.' Bree felt a rising fear
that she had been a gullible fool to leave the flat
with this stranger. While a tiny voice reminded her

dryly that she would have followed him anywhere. 'You don't even look remotely like Reece.'

'He doesn't look like me.' He gave that same cynical smile. 'I suppose I do owe you some proof,' he allowed. 'Wait here.' He entered the other bedroom and returned with the photo of Reece that he had already shown her and a folded document which he passed to her. 'Reece's birth certificate, and here's my driver's licence.'

Bree glanced at the licence showing an address in Fig Tree Pocket, Queensland, and then unfolded the other document and read it. Heath Durant's name was there, and a Pamela Durant. née Andrews. The child registered was Reece Andrew Durant. She glanced up at him as he stood once again looking down at her, hands lightly on his hips, the buttons of his shirt undone at the collar gaping open to reveal the tanned mahogany of his chest and a V of dark hair.

'He took his mother's maiden name,' he said, and she heard an underlying emotion that sounded like bitterness in those softly spoken words. 'Satisfied?'

'But your wife. Mrs Durant.' She stumbled over the title. 'How will she feel about us, Ben and me, landing on her doorstep?'

'Reece's mother died seven years ago,' he said, and took the paper from her, folding it, and tossing it, the licence and the photo aside on to the coffee table.

Nervously uncertain, Bree watched him turn from her and run his hand slowly over the back of his neck as though to ease a nagging tautness. She didn't quite know what to say and part of his tension seemed to take hold of her. Did he still feel the loss of his wife, the mother of his son?

Slowly he turned back to face her and her heartbeats pounded inside her.

'I'm sorry,' she said shakily.

'Are you?' he asked harshly. His whole attitude was more anger than sorrow, she would have sworn it.

'Yes.'

'Don't bother being sorry. Pamela and I——' he paused and a cold mask came down over his face. 'No matter. You'd better get some sleep. It'll be a long day with the baby tomorrow.' He walked away from her and picked up his glass, refilling it from the decanter on the small bartop.

Bree paused at her door to look back at him, but he was staring at a framed seascape on the wall over the bar, his back to her, an air of unapproachability in his stance. She continued into the bedroom, her mind as numb as her body was tired. She couldn't begin to understand this unpredictable, disturbing man or the undercurrents that were so very close to the surface beneath his words, in his tone of voice, in his body tension, that seemed to colour his relationship with his son.

CHAPTER THREE

Now they were heading through the suburbs of Brisbane, having crossed the city from the airport, and the traffic was a little lighter. Heath Durant had taken the wheel of the late model Mercedes, the driver sitting in the passenger seat beside him while Bree shared the back seat with the baby.

Bree wondered what position the middle-aged man held. Bill Roland. Heath had introduced him to her, but had given her no clue as to his status. He could be an employee or a friend judging by the way Heath spoke to him. They used each other's christian names and talked as though they were old friends, and yet there was a slight deference in the older man's attitude.

At any rate, Bill Roland had shown no surprise at seeing her or the baby when he had met their plane, so obviously he had been prepared for them. Bree stifled a yawn and shifted Ben on her lap.

'Not far to go now, young lady,' Bill Roland turned slightly in his seat to speak to her. 'I guess you'll be glad to get the little fellow home?'

'Yes.' Home. Her eyes were drawn to the rear vision mirror and for a couple of seconds locked with those unsettling blue ones. Home. Where the heart is. The hackneyed old saying sprang into her mind out of nowhere. She pulled her eyes unwillingly from their tantalising study of the side of his face, the square firmness of his jaw, the way his dark hair hugged the tanned skin of the back of his neck, a few strands just touching on his collar, the splash of grey-white at his temple. If she wasn't careful Heath Durant would see exactly the state of her heart. In its vulnerable position right on her sleeve.

'Peg's got the nursery all set up and she's as pleased as punch to have a youngster in the house again,' grinned Bill. 'Oh, Peg's the wife,' he explained to Bree. 'I guess you'd say we sort of keep the cogs turning at the old place. I'm chief outdoors and Peg's in charge inside!'

Ben stirred and gave a half cry half yawn and Bill peered over the back of the seat to look at him. 'Sturdy little fellow.' His finger came over to tickle Ben's cheek and the baby grinned happily. 'Can't wait to see Peg's face light up when she sees him.' He beamed at Bree. 'She's a right old softie over babies.'

The Mercedes slowed down and Heath turned it between thick white gateposts, following a tree-lined driveway which curved around in front of the most magnificent house Bree had seen in her life. Ranch style was probably the most accurate way to describe it, but even by modern standards it was huge. Only single-storied, the length of it seemed to go on for ever, and apart from the house was a four-berth garage. The gardens were cleverly landscaped to give the appearance of a natural bush setting and between the garage and the house a large purple bougainvillaea cascaded in riotous splendour.

It was Bill who opened the door of the car for her while Heath disappeared to the boot to unload her luggage, although Bill was quick to take the cardboard cartons Heath handed him. Slowly Bree climbed from the car and stood on the asphalt with Ben in her arms, unable to take her eyes from the dream quality of Heath Durant's home in its beautiful setting.

A long verandah ran the whole length of the front of the house and pot plants hung here and there, cascading ferny greenery, giving the effect of coolness and shade. Spiky red-flowering grevilleas stirred in the breeze, and as they approached the short flight of wide steps to the verandah a couple of honey-eaters protested noisily and moved down to the next shrub. Then the front door was swung open and a woman of about fifty, grey-haired with a broad smiling face, hurried out to greet them.

'Here's Peg,' said Bill unnecessarily.

'You must be Briony.' Peg welcomed her, her eyes only for the baby.

'It's Bree. I . . . I guess it's a nickname that stuck,' she stammered, full up with guilt again, even if what she told them was not exactly an untruth. She had always been called Bree for as long as she could remember. No one had ever called her by her given name, Brianne.

'Then welcome, Bree.' Peg Roland's arms came out automatically for the baby. 'Oh, what a bonnie little mite!' she crooned to him, and Ben, sensing he had found a slave, smiled angelically up at her. 'And what's your name, lovey?'

'Ben,' supplied Bree as Heath walked around the side of the car with her suitcase, followed by Bill with her two cartons.

'Isn't he a lovely little fellow?' Peg appealed to Heath, and at his noncommittal reply her smile faltered just a fraction, her eyes going to Bree, who felt herself flushing. 'Yes, well, come on inside,' she said quickly. 'I've a nice lunch waiting for you, and no doubt this young man could do with his lunch as well. Is he on solids yet?' she asked Bree, leading them into the house.

'If you don't mind looking after the baby for a moment I'll show Bree to her room,' Heath cut in drily, and Bree hastily handed Peg the cooler containing Ben's formula.

'It just needs heating,' she said as she turned to follow Heath's straight back.

'I'll put it on straight away.' Peg disappeared into what must be the kitchen area.

'This way,' said Heath over his shoulder as Bree hurried to catch up with him.

Her eyes grew round at the quietly expensive décor of the house, and it was beautiful, and yet comfortably homely as well. The ceilings were all light varnished pine with heavy darkly stained exposed beams. The living-room was huge, with a polished wood floor, covered here and there by thick furry scatter rugs, giving a cosy rustic welcome. A couple of deep armchairs stood by a large brick feature fireplace and one wall was completely lined with shelves, partially filled with books.

'This is your room.' Heath opened a door down a short hallway from the living-room and stood back for her to enter.

It was most definitely a feminine room, from its very pale apricot walls and flat white ceiling to the deep cream carpet and white Queen Anne style furniture. On the three-quarter-sized bed was a spread of satiny white, patterned with sprays of lemon and apricot flowers and soft green ferns.

'These be all right here on the window seat?' asked Bill, who had followed them into the room carrying the cartons.

'Oh, yes.' Bree roused herself, lost in a sense of admiration.

'This door leads to the bathroom and that's a walk-in closet. Ben's room is right next door.' Heath said, almost absently, as Bill left them. 'I'll leave you to freshen up. Come on through to the dining-room when you're ready.' And he too was gone.

For some minutes she stood where she was and gazed about her in disbelief. It was the most exquisite room she had ever seen, so far removed from Reece and Briony's flat, the ramshackle old house she had shared in Bundaberg, from any room, any house she had been in in her whole life, that she felt like pinching herself to see if she was actually here.

Stepping gingerly across to the closet, she cautiously opened the louvred door. Good grief! Her few dresses would be lost in the huge wardrobe, and she would need only one of the dozen or so drawers to hold her underclothes. The thick pile of the carpet was soft beneath her feet and she trod carefully, thinking she should remove her sandals in case she marked it.

The bathroom was white with feature tiles printed in the same lemon and apricot flower design as the bedspread and the thick bath towels on the gleaming rails were a rich deep green that added a splash of vibrant colour. Bree washed her face and found her lipstick in her bag.

The mirror in the bathroom reflected her face, pale and thin, thinner than she'd realised it was. No wonder he'd thought she hadn't been eating! She looked gaunt and there were dark circles under her eyes. The soft blouse she wore hung on her thin shoulders and her skirt looked as though it didn't belong to her.

In her eyes, her shabby appearance seemed to be
magnified by the grandeur of the beautiful room,
and she felt a rush of unease, a sudden panic, that
she didn't fit in here, she was out of her
environment, that she had no right to be here.

She hurried out of the bathroom, stopping in
the middle of the bedroom, her eyes going to the
battered old suitcase and then to the cartons on
the window seat. Slowly she walked over to them,
so incongruous in the midst of such luxury, and
reached out and touched them as if to reassure
herself that this was Bree Ransome in the middle
of another world. Not a fantasy, for real.

Leaning forward, she took a gulp of steadying
air and gazed out through the window between
white gossamer cross-over curtains. Then she saw
that the house was built on a rise and that the land
sloped gently downwards, and through the trees
she glimpsed the river. The grass was neatly
trimmed but most of the trees were natural, gums
tall and straight, a few pines and she-oaks, giving a
setting of shady bushland. The allotment must be
huge, she thought, and she could see no other
neighbouring houses, although they might have
been screened by the trees.

It was all so very beautiful. Not even in her
wildest daydreams could she have imagined
anything so quietly opulent, and yet so unpretenti-
ous. And to think Reece had never so much as
hinted that this was the kind of life he was used to,
in which he had been raised. It was so different
from theirs, hers and Briony's, that there was no
parallel.

'Are you ready for lunch?' His deep voice from
the doorway made her start and she swung around
to face him a little guiltily.

'Yes. I'm sorry, I was just looking at the view. It's beautiful.'

'It is that.' His eyes never left her face.

'Have you lived here long?' Her body felt suddenly burning hot as though his hands instead of his eyes moved over her.

'I had the house built about six years ago.'

After his wife's death. Then Pamela Durant had never lived here. Her eyes fell to her hands in case he should see the jumble of emotions in their clear grey depths. 'I can't understand why Reece would have wanted to leave all this.'

'Can't you?'

Bree shook her head, the back light from the window catching the edges of her hair, forming a bright outline around her face.

'My son, Miss Ransome, sees me as the original capitalist pig. Reece has a scorn for the money he's never been without.' He shoved his hands deep into his pockets and frowned. 'I had hoped being without funds would cure him, but obviously it didn't teach him the lesson I thought it would. Perhaps I underestimated him.'

'Reece never seemed to care much about money,' Bree shrugged. 'He always managed to get by.'

'Did he have a steady job?'

'Not exactly,' she replied carefully. 'He had occasional engagements with various bands, but apart from that I guess he must have had unemployment benefits.'

'You didn't know where his money came from?' He was regarding her thoughtfully, if somewhat sceptically.

'We didn't discuss money,' was all she could find to answer him, and she shifted her stance uneasily as he continued to watch her. 'Reece never flashed his money around, but he never seemed to be broke or anything,' she finished lamely, wishing she could know what he was thinking behind those lash-shielded eyes.

'Let's have lunch,' he said after a moment, changing the subject, and glanced down at his wristwatch. 'I have to get back to the airport.'

'The airport?' Bree halted in mid-stride, her eyes springing to his face as a tide of alarm washed over her.

'I have appointments in Sydney this afternoon. I still have some unfinished business to attend to down there.'

'You mean you . . . I'm to stay here by myself?' Bree stammered.

'Hardly by yourself.' He raised one dark eyebrow. 'Peg and Bill live in the house. They have a flat through the kitchen.'

Bree could only stare at him.

'Peg will be pleased to give you a hand with the baby.' He smiled faintly.

'I thought you'd be here, too,' she said softly. 'How long will you be in Sydney?'

'Ten days. A week at least.'

'Ten days?' The thought of not seeing him was a sudden pain inside her and she fought to keep some measure of control, to guard her expression. She barely knew this man. He was a virtual stranger and the feelings he aroused within her frightened her. She wanted to reach out to him, cling to him, but that of course was out of the question. 'Oh!' she breathed, her eyes falling.

And she could feel his eyes burning her again, feel the poised tension in his stance, and her gaze was drawn irresistibly upwards to meet his. How long they stood like that, tensed, tuned to each other, not touching but sensing every emotive nuance in each other, Bree couldn't have told, but Heath was the first to move, to break the spell that bound them. Turning suddenly away from her, he held the door open, motioning her to precede him, his face now coldly set, uncompromising, and Bree walked shakily past him and into the hallway.

For those first few days Bree felt a little intrusive with Peg Roland, but the older woman showed such open friendliness that gradually Bree began to relax. Together they fell into an easy companionship and a shared routine with Ben, who thrived contentedly under their care. Although she didn't notice it herself, so did Bree begin to feel more like her old self. She regained the weight she had shed and her face lost its gauntness. Her time spent in the garden happily helping Bill soon tanned her skin and bleached her fair hair to an even lighter sheen.

It was two full weeks before they heard from Heath Durant. In his absence Bree felt she had managed to get him into some realistic perspective. She told herself it was only natural that a man as attractive, as worldly, as he undoubtedly was, should make such an impact on her. For hadn't he made an appearance in her life when she was most likely to be impressed, when her customary equilibrium had been out of balance? And was it any wonder that it was upset, with the shock of her sister's callous behaviour, with having the responsibility of caring for Ben, and then her horrifying experience with Max Turner. She still woke up nights in blind terror at the memory of that.

Heath Durant's materialisation would have done proud the very best knight in shining armour rescuing a damsel in distress, she thought wryly. The whole episode could only show him in the most admirable light. Why wouldn't she be completely bowled over? Physically, that was.

As a person she knew absolutely nothing about him. All her instincts tried to tell her his character was impeccable, but if life had taught her one thing it was that appearances could be deceptive, that people were not always what they seemed. Her own sister was a prime example of that.

Her only source of information about Heath Durant was Peg, and only very occasionally, Bill. More often than not Bree worked alongside Bill in the garden in companionable silence. That Bill held his employer in the highest esteem was quite obvious, but he wasn't one to gossip about him.

Peg, on the other hand, loved to chat, although she was never malicious. From Peg Bree learned that Heath owned one of the largest and most successful construction companies in the state. He had inherited the small business from his father-in-law and had expanded it from a minor suburban firm into a multi-million-dollar concern that provided jobs for many hundreds of workers on sites as far north as Cairns.

Peg and Bill had been with Heath for nearly fifteen years, which meant that they must have known his wife, Pamela, but not once did Peg so much as mention her name. Surprisingly she had little to say about Reece, and Bree couldn't bring herself to ask questions. She would feel she was prying.

When Heath telephoned, they were cooking, Peg making scones while Bree watched and helped with the clearing of the dishes. Peg's hands were covered in flour, so it was Bree who lifted the receiver.

'Bree?' His voice seemed even deeper on the phone and so blatantly masculine that she turned slightly away from Peg to hide the blush that washed over her cheeks.

'Yes, it is. Hello,' she said breathily, her knuckles white where she gripped the mouthpiece.

'Heath Durant here.' He sounded a little brusque as though he was in a hurry. 'Is Peg handy?'

As if he'd needed to tell her who he was, Bree grimaced. 'Yes, she's right here doing some baking. Do you want to talk to her?'

'No, don't disturb her.' There was a faint pause. 'How are you settling in?' His voice was flat and she couldn't glean a clue to his expression.

'Fine, thank you.' Bree searched for something else to say. 'Ben cut another tooth,' she added, and cringed inwardly. What on earth had made her say that? He wouldn't care about something as mundane as a baby's tooth.

'Did he now?' There was a softer edge to his voice that could have been amusement. 'I hope he didn't have you walking the floor?'

'Oh no. He was very good. He always is,' she replied quickly. 'Peg says he's the best behaved baby she's ever seen.'

'High praise,' he remarked, and she wondered if he was laughing at her.

'Did you want me to give Peg a message?' she asked stiffly.

'If you wouldn't mind. Tell her I don't expect to be back until early next week.'

'Oh.' That was still at least five days away. 'I'll tell her.'

'Thanks.' There was a pause again and Bree nervously twisted the phone cord in her fingers. 'I'll see you next week,' he said then, and the receiver buzzed in her ear.

Slowly Bree replaced it on its cradle, her heart thudding in her breast. Well, she certainly had herself sorted out where Heath Durant was concerned. So much for her rationalisation! She could be so very analytical when he was away, and yet the mere sound of his voice had her blushing like a schoolgirl, her heart fluttering like a candle in the wind.

'Heath?' Peg raised her eyebrows enquiringly as she turned from sliding a tray of scones into the oven.

'Yes. He said to tell you he won't be back until next week.' Bree picked up the mixing bowl and carried it across to the dishwasher.

'Tsk! This is turning out to be a long trip for him, and he so enjoys being home, too.' She shook her head. 'He works far too hard. I was just saying to Bill the other night, he does the work of two men and rarely takes the time to relax.'

She glanced across to Bree. 'When he told me you and the baby were coming to stay I was that pleased. I thought he might take a bit of time away from the rat race of the business world. And I'm still hoping. Once he gets this problem with the suppliers down south worked out I'm sure you'll see more of him—don't you worry now.'

Bree stood staring open-mouthed at the older woman. Surely she couldn't think that Heath and ... that they were ... 'Oh, Peg, I really don't expect him to bother about us. It's enough, much more than enough, that he's taken us into his home.'

'And I should think he would. Heath has never shirked a responsibility in his life,' Peg stated.

'But I never asked him to be responsible for us. He didn't even find out about Ben until the night before he brought us here.'

'I don't know—you young girls, so independent these days. Bringing up a child on your own is not easy when you've no one to support you. You let Heath take care of you. You need some looking after, I could tell that the moment I set eyes on you.' Peg waved a spoon expressively. 'Why, since you've been here you've really picked up. Heath will notice the difference, you take it from me. Now, how long have those scones been in the oven? I forgot to set the timer.'

There was no way Bree could find to put Peg in the picture. She had imagined that when Heath Durant had told the Rolands that he was bringing the two of them to stay for a while he would have explained their relationship. Obviously he hadn't, and she could understand it that he might not want it made public that Ben was his grandson, but surely he would know what other connotations would be put on it.

Bree sighed. If she tried to explain, and she would only be able to safely tell half of the story, then she knew she would begin to trip herself up. So she said nothing. Better to let Heath do the explaining. When he came home she'd make a point of insisting that he did so. That Peg should think she had had an affair with Heath Durant and that Ben was his son, and hers, made her blush all over.

Friday was the Rolands' wedding anniversary,

and it was a yearly ritual that they went in to the city to a top restaurant to celebrate the occasion. They'd never missed in thirty-five years, Bill told Bree. But this year Peg was reluctant to go as it meant leaving Bree and the baby alone in the house for the evening.

Seeing the disappointment on Bill's face, Bree hurriedly assured Peg that she'd be fine. She'd watch television or read, and Ben was never any trouble at night. Peg couldn't miss her anniversary dinner.

After much persuasion Peg agreed to go, and with the house to herself Bree fed and settled Ben and then made herself a light snack to eat in front of the television. She watched the news and a frivolous game show before clearing away her dinner dishes. However, she couldn't seem to settle to any of the following TV programmes, and after persevering with a detective story that irritated rather than intrigued she switched off the set and decided to have a leisurely bath.

The house was quiet with scarcely the creak of contracting timber when she eventually returned to the living-room, her thin towelling bathrobe over her short cotton nightdress. She'd read for an hour or so and then have an early night.

Settling down in one of the large armchairs by the empty fireplace—it was still too warm for a fire—she picked up the much publicised best-seller she had borrowed from Peg. She had switched off the main living-room lights and only a bright standard lamp encircled her with light.

The book was fast moving and she became engrossed, unconsciously settling more comfortably into the chair, her legs draped over one softly padded arm, her back braced against the other. Once she glanced at her wristwatch to see that it was only nine o'clock, but at some stage after that she fell asleep.

Or perhaps she was just dozing, for she was half conscious that she was dreaming. Isolated incidents from her past surfaced in her memory, scenes of various families, in different places, of herself and Briony only children, in one of the foster-homes she remembered. It hadn't been the first one for they had lived with at least five different families during the twelve years they had been wards of the State, but it was the one she seemed to have the most vivid memories of. The family that fostered them lived on a farm somewhere outside Brisbane, and both Briony and Bree had had to work for their keep. They were expected to do so. The people had four children of their own and Bree knew that their own children had had to work just as hard. But it had been pleasant, the smooth warmth of the soft-eyed cows in the milking sheds, the smell of the newly reaped fodder paddocks. When the farm was sold Bree and Briony had gone to another family farther north in Bundaberg.

During the next few years Briony had seemed to change. She was always in and out of trouble and had even been the cause of one of their changes of family. When Bree managed to get a job as a shop assistant and they had moved into a small flat that was the first home of their own, Briony had settled down for a while.

Then it had started again. She refused to try to get a job and was even caught by the police in a car driven at high speeds by a youth who had no licence. Bree tried to draw her away from the crowd she mixed with, who seemed to jaunt from one hotel to another drinking until they passed out.

At one such party one weekend Briony had met Reece, a guitarist in a band hired for the evening, and she had fallen head over heels in love with him. Almost right away, after a heated argument with Bree, Briony had gone to live with him, moving on with him when the band decided to try to make the big time in Sydney, and she had made no effort to contact Bree until she was pregnant.

Bree remembered again her horror at the dinginess of the flat her sister shared with Reece, and with reluctance she had stayed, taking the small second bedroom, when Briony begged her not to leave her, saying she couldn't go through having the baby on her own. It was all bearable until Max Turner came home one night with Reece.

Bree shuddered in her sleep. How she had disliked him! From the moment she met him. And then the night he had pushed his way into the flat. She felt again his hands on her breasts and she moaned agitatedly fighting to get away from him. Her body felt stiff and she panicked, thinking she couldn't move. Her book, falling to the floor with a thud, woke her up.

Half awake, she blinked up at the unfamiliar ceiling with its pine panelling and dark exposed beams, and as she turned her head a figure was looming over her, moving forward, indistinct in the shadows outside the circle of light from the reading lamp.

Bree screamed in terror. No, not again! Please, not again! She couldn't bear it. Hands were reaching out for her, catching her flailing arms as she began to fight him, pinning them to her body, and she gulped another breath.

It was some moments after the sound of an

angry exclamation filtered through to her panic-stricken mind that she realised she was not in the dingy flat in Sydney, that the dark head backlit above her and the firm hands gripping her arms were not, in fact, Max Turner's.

CHAPTER FOUR

BREE slumped back against the chair and closed her eyes, the fight drained out of her. 'I'm sorry, I was dreaming and I thought . . .' Her eyelids fluttered open as her voice faded away.

He remained there leaning over her, close enough for her to distinguish his features. How could she ever have mistaken him for Max Turner?

'I can imagine what you thought,' he remarked drily, but gently for all that. 'I'm also beginning to wonder if you really needed my help back in Sydney.' The corners of his mouth lifted momentarily and Bree actually felt her heart turn over under the devastation of that half smile.

His hands were still on her arms and his touch burned, excited, flowed life through her strength-sapped body.

'Did I hurt you?' Her voice sounded unlike her own, her senses reeling from the extremes of emotion. Fear. Repulsion. Attraction. Temptation.

'No.' He hadn't moved, continued to look down at her, his eyes going to her trembling lips, and her tongue-tip came nervously out to moisten them, feeling her mouth tingle as though he'd covered her lips with his own.

At the same moment Heath's eyes narrowed, his expression shielded by his dark-lashed lids, and the pressure of his fingers tightened on her arms. That same tension was there again, building up between them, and Bree's heart began a heavy thudding in her ears as she caught her breath, waiting for his next move.

How she wanted him to take her in his arms, hold her close, have his lips kiss her mouth, her throat. She felt herself go hot and cold all over and when those same hands lifted her out of the chair her heart almost stopped beating. However, once she was upright his hands fell away and her knees sagged so that he reached for her again, steadying her. Involuntarily her hand went to his chest as she regained her balance and beneath her hand she felt his own heartbeat's acceleration.

Startled, her gaze flew to his face and then shied away from the glow that had begun to smoulder in his blue eyes, now dark pools of fire, to fall to his lips, seeing them tighten as his muscular body tensed. He had shed his suit coat, had removed his tie, and his pale shirt, the material feeling like silk beneath her fingers, was open part way down his chest, his tanned skin only millimetres from her fingertips. If she moved her hand . . . Bree drew a quick steadying breath.

Then she was standing alone and Heath's long legs had put space between them as he stooped to retrieve her fallen book and handed it to her. Her fingers reached out and clutched at the book for dear life, feeling as though she'd fall over if she let it go.

How she wished she was more experienced, more competent at hiding her feelings. She knew the expression on her face gave her away. Just then she had all but thrown herself at him. He couldn't have failed to read the invitation in her eyes, her face, her whole body. And the invitation had been refused. She flushed with hurt embarrassment.

'Looks like you've lost your place.' He had

moved away, across the furry white sheepskin rug,
and she slowly raised her head to look at him. He
was half turned from her, hand reaching for the
ornate cigarette box on the mantelpiece above the
fireplace.

'It doesn't matter. I'll find it again,' she said, all
her instincts telling her to leave him now, but she
doubted she could get her legs to move.
Somewhere between the signal box in her mind
and her motor system there was a messy traffic
jam of thoughts and sensations that she was trying
desperately to unravel.

'We weren't expecting you back until next
week,' she managed to say as she stood in the
same place, her hands still locked on her book.
'You said on the phone that you——' Bree
stopped. She had no right to comment on his
comings and goings.

'Things moved faster than I'd anticipated.' He
flicked his lighter and the flame briefly highlighted
the planes and angles of his face. He drew on the
cigarette and turned back to face her. 'I thought
everyone was in bed and I was heading for the
kitchen to make myself a cup of coffee when I
heard you say something. I didn't realise you were
talking in your sleep.'

'I guess I dozed off.' Bree put the book on the
chair and forced herself to take a few steps. 'I'll . . .
if you'd like I'll make you some coffee. Would you
like something to eat? An omelette, or some
toasted sandwiches?'

'An omelette would be good.' He flexed his
shoulders tiredly. 'I didn't have time to eat before
the plane left and the flight didn't serve meals.'

'All right. It won't take long.' Bree hurried into
the kitchen. Working with Peg these past two

weeks had at least taught her the layout of the kitchen and she found the utensils and ingredients she needed without too much trouble.

As she began to whisk the eggs she looked up to see him sitting at the small breakfast bar watching her. 'Will ham and cheese be all right?' she asked, her stomach feeling much like the beaten eggs.

'Fine.' He glanced at his wristwatch. 'Peg and Bill are having an early night.'

'Oh, they've gone into the city for dinner and a show,' she told him. 'It's their wedding anniversary today.'

'The fifteenth. So it is,' he said softly, his eyes watching her through the curling wisp of smoke from his cigarette.

The fact that they were here in the house alone together came suddenly back to Bree, and her mouth went dry, the tension returning threefold. Was he aware of their isolation, the tension, too? Could he *not* be aware of it?

Bree shot a look at him through her lashes and then wished she hadn't. For his eyes were on her, lit with a brooding sensuality that had her heart pounding again. No one before had affected her this way. Never in her life had she been so conscious of a man, so physically honed to his presence.

And it wasn't that she was naïve and inexperienced about life, she told herself. Even though she hadn't slept around like so many of the girls she knew, like her own sister, she wasn't blind to the existence of physical relationships. She had been out with quite a few young men, had even fancied she'd begun to care about a couple of them, but when the crunch came and the inevitable 'If you really loved me you'd . . .' she had always opted out, knowing instinctively that love meant something far different to her than it did to them. Making love without loving wasn't for her. It had to be with love. She couldn't settle for anything less.

Turning back to the stove, Bree poured the omelette mixture into the non-stick frying-pan. Her thoughts ricocheted back to those moments just after she had realised it was Heath Durant leaning over her. The intense wanting, a burning need to be gathered into his arms, to be caressed, to be kissed. And it was this overwhelming yearning with which she'd never before had to cope.

If he had wanted to make love to her there and then would she have . . .? Bree felt a blush rush over her cheeks and she almost shook with the strength of her feelings, a jumble of desire, of self-derision, of indecision.

This aloneness was far too volatile, the silence too tension-filled. She had to say something to lighten it, to bring some measure of normality. She glanced back at Heath as he sat still openly watching her, his expression not giving a clue to his thoughts.

'Shall I pour you some coffee while you're waiting for the omelette to cook?' she asked him stiltedly.

'Please.' He stubbed out his cigarette in the ashtray by his elbow and folded back the cuffs of his shirt over his tanned forearms. 'I feel as if I've been awake for a week,' he said, and rubbed a hand over the slight beard-roughness of his jaw.

'Did your . . . your trip end up all right?' Bree asked as she set the steaming mug of coffee in front of him and retreated to the stove to tend to the omelette.

'Better than I'd expected, but not as good as it should have,' he replied, and took a sip of his coffee. 'Mmm, that's good.'

'You were having trouble with the supply of materials weren't you?' Bree prompted and Heath's coffee mug halted halfway to his mouth as he raised a surprised eyebrow. 'Peg told . . . she said you were having trouble with . . .' Bree stammered. 'I'm sorry, I didn't mean to pry,' she finished apologetically.

Heath shrugged. 'Peg loves to talk.' His eyes regarded her steadily.

'Oh, she never said anything about—er— anything. I mean, we weren't gossiping exactly.' Bree fumbled with the frying-pan as she slipped the omelette on to a plate. 'She said you have a construction company.'

He nodded his thanks for the omelette and began to eat, making short work of the meal.

'Peg only told me because—well——' Bree swallowed nervously, wishing she'd let the conversation drop.

'Because?'

'I guess because she thinks we're . . . we're friends.' She swung away and stacked the frying-pan and the mixing bowl into the dishwasher.

'Friends?' he queried expressionlessly.

'Yes. Well, that we've known each other for some time,' she improvised guiltily.

'I wonder what gave her that idea?' he asked softly, and Bree turned slowly around to face him.

There was a cynicism in the set of his lips, the cold blue-greyness of his eyes. He slid off the stool and walked around the breakfast counter and into the kitchen, casually opening the dishwasher and putting his empty plate inside.

He was close enough to touch. If she lent a fraction to the side the contact her body seemed to crave would be made. Surely he must hear the heavy thudding of her heart, feel the wave of physical attraction?

'I wonder what gave her that idea?' His words made her stomach turn over. He couldn't think that she'd lead Peg to believe they were more than the virtual strangers they were.

'I don't know what you mean,' she said, forcing herself to stand her ground and not give in to the alarm-filled urge to flee from him.

'Don't you? If I know Peg she would have been dying to discover how the land lies.' He leant back against the counter top, still far too close for her comfort.

'I would have thought you'd have explained it to her when you told her you were bringing us here,' Bree said softly, beginning to edge slowly away from him.

'I don't need to explain myself to anyone, let alone Peg,' Heath replied coldly, folding his arms across the solidity of his chest.

The arrogance of his tone, his attitude, struck a chord of anger in Bree. He was so damnably sure of himself, with no thought for the feelings of others, and she heard herself speak before she could draw rein on her tongue.

'Not even if you know people are going to misconstrue the situation?'

With one light movement he straightened from his relaxed stance against the counter too and his hands were now resting on his hips, solid and inflexible, his eyes boring down on her. 'In what way?' he asked quietly.

Already Bree was regretting her brief spurt of

impulsiveness, and she turned away from him, shrugging nervously. 'It doesn't matter.'

'If it doesn't matter,' he repeated, 'then why bring it up at all?'

'I . . . It's nothing. I'm . . . I'm tired. I think I'll go to bed.' She went to move away, make her escape, but his hand came out to clasp her upper arm, impeding her progress, turning her easily back to face him.

'In what way and by whom has the situation been misconstrued?' he persisted.

Bree clasped her hands tightly together, her eyes cast downwards. But her eyes had great difficulty focusing on her hands when his body was so close to her. Her eyes went involuntarily to the silk material of his shirt resting tautly over his flat stomach, the shine of his gold belt buckle, the dark material of his trousers that moulded the firm muscles of his thighs.

Her heart began to race again and she swallowed convulsively. She was so totally enmeshed in the web of magnetism he wove unconsciously about him that it frightened her.

His finger lifted her chin, made her eyes meet his. 'Well, Bree?'

'I told you, it was nothing. Nobody. I don't want to talk about it,' she got out, while her traitorous body, that seemed not to belong to her, burned to feel the hard contours of his along its entire length, free, uninhibited, without reservation.

'As far as I know you've only seen Peg and Bill since I've been away. That narrows it down to two. So, we wait up for Peg and Bill and we ask them to explain this,' he paused, 'misconstruction.'

'You . . . wouldn't!' she whispered chokedly.

'Wouldn't I? I assure you I would,' he said levelly, his voice edged in steel.

Looking up at him, at the calm resolution of his expression, she knew she would be no match for the strength of purpose he exuded. He would do as he said and not suffer a shred of the embarrassment she would experience while he questioned the other woman.

'Peg thinks that Ben's your son,' she said in a rush, before she lost her nerve. 'Everyone will think so.'

Heath made no comment for pregnant seconds and the ticking of the clock seemed to pound loudly in Bree's ears. She glanced up at him through the shield of her lashes.

'I don't give a damn what everyone thinks,' he stated at last. 'I gave up caring what other people think probably before you were born.' His eyes held hers with compelling intensity. 'So Peg thinks you're my mistress?' A cynical smile pulled one corner of his mouth.

Colour flooded Bree's throat and washed over her cheeks. His words, delivered in that cold sardonic tone, seemed deliberately disparaging.

'And you do care what people think?' he queried with humourless amusement.

'Of course!' she burst out indignantly.

His harsh laugh made her jump. 'But not enough to have an illegitimate child by my son?' he asked cruelly, and his fingers tightened on her arm until she flinched at the pain he was causing, unable to find an answer.

'What would you have me do? Take out an advertisement in the daily newspaper? Heath Durant wants it known that he is not the father of Miss Bree Ransome's child.'

'No! Why are you saying all this?' Bree appealed to him. 'I don't see any need to tell anyone else. But Peg's different. And Bill. They live here. Peg thinks . . . she thinks we . . .'

'Cohabit?' he finished brutally. 'Or are you more familiar with the term "sleep together"?'

'Please stop this.' Bree pulled away from him, but his fingers held her in a vicelike grip. 'You're hurting my arm! Let me go!'

He relaxed some of the punishing pressure but didn't release her. 'Then you want me to tell Peg we don't sleep together?'

'Well, I . . . maybe she doesn't think we sleep together now,' Bree's heartbeats rose to choke her and she swallowed steadyingly, wishing she could get away from him, have done with this dreadful conversation. 'But perhaps she thinks that once we . . . well, because of Ben she . . .' Her voice gave out on her.

'Oh. Only once.' He raised a dark eyebrow. 'How unlucky for us,' he remarked sarcastically. 'And I allowed it to happen. I should have known better, wouldn't you say? I mean, being old enough to be your father, that is.'

'Please don't say that.'

'Please don't say what, specifically?' he continued his torment.

'That you're old enough to be my father. You don't . . . you don't seem to be that old to me,' she finished softly.

'Oh, I assure you, I am. More than old enough.' The last was said in a tone that vibrated huskily through her, firing her senses to an almost unbearable pitch.

She stood looking up at him and she felt the rigidness of the control he was undoubtedly exerting over himself, recognising how close to breaking the surface it was. And in his tension was an anger. She wished she could begin to understand the reason for it, for she knew instinctively that it was self-directed and far more complex, running much too deep to be blamed on their superficial conversation.

Bree's lips were dry and she automatically touched them with the tip of her tongue again. As she watched his eyes changed colour, burned with hot blue fires that raged out of control over her face, cascading downwards to the agitated rise and fall of her unconfined breasts beneath the thin covering of her nightdress and bathrobe.

His naked scrutiny charged the air about them, and everything faded from Bree's vision into a fuzzy backdrop for the chiselled face above her. He could have been an exquisite sculpture etched from solid mahogany and she drank in the sharp angles of his cheekbones and jaw, the furrows engraved on either side of his mouth, the straight proud nose with nostrils now slightly flared, and his mouth. God! She couldn't drag her eyes from the sensuousness of his lips. She wanted to taste them, to feel them on hers, plundering, and her stomach plummeted.

'God—Bree!' The tortured words broke from him and he pulled her roughly against him, his arms capturing her there as though he never intended to surrender her. 'Fatherly is the last thing I feel,' he said raggedly.

His lips were against her temple, moved down over the side of her face, found the sensitivity of her earlobe, and she moaned with startled pleasure. And her own lips, of their own accord, were kissing the line of his jaw, searching almost desperately for the feel of his lips upon them.

At last his mouth found hers and they clung together, their passion running free, their bodies arching until Bree could feel every hard arousing contour of his maleness.

His hand played up the length of her spine his fingers moving through the curtain of fair silky hair to find her nape, holding her head at just the right angle for his marauding mouth. But it was a mutual marauding. For Bree was responding with an abandoned fire she hadn't suspected could possess her.

Spontaneously, her soft lips opened to his and her fingers twined around his neck, delighting in the thick vitality of his dark hair. His breathing was as laboured as her own as his lips covered her face with kisses, sought the creamy curve of her throat.

Fumbling with the small buttons, Bree's fingers slid inside his shirt, over the smooth dampness of his midriff, through the tiny curls of dark hair on his chest, as her lips pressed into the hard muscular column of his neck. The faint musky scent of him tantalised her nostrils and her small even white teeth gently nibbled his tanned skin.

When his hand cupped her swelling breast Bree felt her legs turn to water, could barely support her. His thumb easily found the erect peak of her nipple through the thinness of her nightdress and she groaned against his shoulder, completely intoxicated by the exhilaration of the sensations he was creating. Ecstatic waves of pure pleasure flowed downwards as his fingers teased her burgeoning breasts.

Her whole body cried out for him, demanded a complete capitulation, the ultimate unity, and she knew she was incapable of denying him. Her bathrobe fell to the floor and his lips found the throbbing pulse at the base of her throat, slid over the roundness of her shoulder, pushing aside the thin strap of her nightdress. Then his lips covered the hardness of her naked nipple and she cried out his name, her fingers winding in his hair, not wanting him to cease his sensual assault.

This was madness, she told herself. But it was such divine, indescribable madness. While part of her was horrified at her unresisting submission there was no way she could draw back now. She was his for the taking and he couldn't help but be so very aware of it.

Heath's kisses, his caresses, had set aflame her untouched responses, and no matter how much she tried to warn herself that he was a man so totally experienced, so unlike any she had met before, her perfidious body held the upper hand and was exalting unashamedly in his lovemaking.

'Bree, I want you,' he whispered huskily against her ear, sending shafts of pure craving for complete satisfaction through her. 'But I guess you can feel that.' He gave a soft laugh as he moved sensually against her, turning her knees to water so that she sagged against him, her hands on his body her only support.

'This is a hell of a place to . . .' His lips slid across her cheek to her mouth, drawn irresistibly there, and he kissed her with an all-consuming desire.

With no thought of resistance Bree clung to him, her heartbeats thudding in her breast.

'Come on, let's find more comfortable surroundings.' He swung her easily into his arms and went to stride out of the kitchen.

'No. Heath, I . . .' Bree's hand went to the

solidness of his bare chest and the answering hammering of his heartbeats was almost her undoing. 'We shouldn't,' she whispered almost inaudibly, flushing as she lifted her nightdress back over her breast. 'I . . . my bathrobe.'

His eyes smouldered as he bent to take her trembling lips again, drowning her brief nervous quiver of doubt.

'I'll buy you another one, a hundred others.' He laughed deep in his chest and Bree trembled at the blatantly masculine sound.

'But Peg . . . she'll see it and she'll wonder . . . she'll think . . .' she stammered.

He gave that same cyncial smile. 'And she'll think I took it off you and dropped it there before I carried you into the bedroom and made love to you,' he finished huskily, and set her down. 'We can't have that, can we?' He gave a half smile and picked up the discarded bathrobe with a flourish, the fire still burning in his eyes belying his mocking expression. Draping the robe about her shoulders, he pulled the material on either side of her, propelling her close against him, his lips crushing hers with a passion that made her quiver, as she responded with a feverish fervour.

She was swung up into his arms again and he had taken a couple of steps out of the kitchen when the flash of headlights skittered along the front of the house. Bree felt Heath's body tense beneath her, and even as he paused a car door slammed and footsteps climbed the front steps.

Panic-stricken, Bree struggled in Heath's arms and when they tightened about her she drew a shivering breath.

'Please, Heath! Someone's coming. It must be Peg. Please put me down!' Her hand pushed

ineffectually against the rock wall of his chest and
his eyes were glittering embers as they slanted
down at her. With seeming slow motion he let her
slide over the hardness of his body to the floor. As
the sound of the key turning in the lock echoed
down the short hallway Bree struggled her arms
into the sleeves of her bathrobe, wrapping it
protectively around her as Peg's figure entered the
house, her hand flicking on the hall light.

The older woman turned and caught sight of
Bree and Heath standing there in front of her, and
she gave a start of fright. 'Good gracious, you did
give me a turn!' Her hand went to her heart over
the floral jacket of her best outfit. 'I must say we
were surprised to see your car when we drove in,
Heath. We weren't expecting you till next week.'

'No. I'm pleased to be back sooner than I
anticipated,' he replied easily.

Bree glanced at him out of the corner of her eye
and felt her cheeks glow. He had made no attempt
to rebutton his shirt and it was hanging out of the
waistband of his trousers. His dark hair was
slightly dishevelled from the exploration of her
fingers and she guiltily ran her hand over her own
hair, suspecting it was probably in the same state.

'Did you enjoy your evening?' Heath was asking
easily.

'Oh, yes. It was lovely.' Peg's sharp eyes went
from her employer to Bree, making Bree feel even
more uncomfortable. 'The meal was delicious—I
couldn't fault it. And it makes me feel nice and
spoiled not having to do the dishes afterwards. Bill
enjoyed it, too. He's just putting the car away.
Would you like some coffee, Heath?'

'No, thanks, Peg.' Heath moved towards the
door. 'Bree made me some. I'll go out and put my

car away while Bill's got the garage open.' His
hand was jangling the car keys in his pocket as he
left them.

'Well! Fancy Heath getting back so soon,'
remarked Peg. 'Has he been home long?'

'No, I don't think so. I'm not sure what time he
arrived. I was reading and I'd dozed off.' And
after that time could have raced away or stopped
dead for all she had known. Bree felt as though
Heath's kisses were visible all over her and she
shrank with embarrassment. Peg's indulgent,
knowing smile didn't help at all.

'It's nice that he has you and the baby to come
home to,' she beamed. 'It's a lonely life for a man
without his family about him.'

'Yes. Well, he said his meetings finished sooner
than he expected.' Bree tried to explain and
swallowed embarrassedly. 'I was just going to bed,
so I'll say goodnight. I'm glad you had a nice
time.'

Bree thankfully made her escape, the effort of
walking slowly and not breaking into a headlong
run leaving her weak as she closed her bedroom
door and leant back against it.

Would he come to her? Bree shivered uncontrollably, her sensitised nerve ends reacting with that
same fire Heath had lit. He wanted her, that was
indisputable, and she had ached, still ached, for
him in a way that made her elated and yet fearful
and unsure.

Until tonight in Heath Durant's arms she had
had no trouble at all preserving her ideals, the
ideals that were all tied up and interwoven with
being in love, being loved, and for ever. Now
Heath had shown her another less tractable facet
of her character, one that frightened her.

She wiped a shaking hand across her eyes, surprised to find her brow was damp with perspiration, and she could feel her jaw tense with the effort of controlling her chattering teeth.

Vaguely she heard him start his car, back it into the garage and then close the garage doors with a subdued click. He would be coming inside and . . . Bree walked unsteadily across to her bed, slipping out of her robe and climbing beneath the cool sheets. He would soon be back, and he would come to her, slide his long hard body along the length of hers and meet this burning ache inside her, assuage it, appease it with an expertise she knew instinctively he would possess.

She felt herself blush hotly at her wanton thoughts, wondering why she felt no shame. She had an unclear feeling that she should be remorseful, but how could it be wrong when it felt so very right?

And suddenly she knew why she had drawn away from the fumbling caresses of other men. Heath Durant was the reason why. Somehow she had known all along that when she met that special man it would feel right, for when you loved someone that made it right.

Loved someone? Bree sat bolt upright in her bed. She didn't love this man. She couldn't possibly. She barely knew him. You didn't fall in love so quickly. It was laughable, ludicrous. He was an attractive man, older than the men she had associated with before, and what was more, he was experienced. No man as attractive, as magnetic, as Heath Durant so obviously was, and in his apparently successful position, got to be thirty-seven years old without having women throwing themselves at him. Hadn't she just done that herself?

And if he was looking for some equivalent experience in herself then he would be sadly disappointed. The sum total of her experience was a few unexciting kisses, more experimental than passionate, that she had pulled away from before they'd had a chance to become more than that.

Although the way she had responded to him had to have given him a totally misleading impression. But when he kissed her her instincts took over, her passion rising to match his, any resistance scattering to the four winds.

Her fingers clutched at the bedclothes. Perhaps she was no better than she had accused Briony of being. And look where that sort of life had got her sister! Moving from one dingy flat to another, living life on a tightrope as she pandered to Reece's moods, terrified that he would find another girl. And bringing a child into the world, a child that hadn't really been wanted, had been abandoned just as easily as Briony would have left a pet she'd tired of.

Ben. Oh, no! She had completely forgotten the implications of the baby. Heath thought Ben was hers, that she'd conceived him, borne him, and therefore there would be no question of her experience. And there was certainly no question of Heath's experience. If she allowed him to make love to her then he would know it was impossible for Ben to be hers. He would know she had lied to him.

And what would he do then? Send her away and not let her see Ben again? Or perhaps send them both away? Surely he wouldn't be so callous. She shivered. A man like Heath Durant would not allow the emotional pleas of someone who had deceived him cloud any decision he made, she knew that.

The web of deception was entangling her further, wrapping her in a prison-like cocoon from which she would soon be unable to escape. Maybe it would be better if she cut her losses now, turned and ran before she got in any deeper, at least before she jeopardised Ben's position. Heath Durant could give Ben a far better life than she could ever hope to give him, she was in no doubt about that. She didn't even have a job to support them, and what little money she had left might be made to stretch out for three weeks or so. Her head sank wearily on to her hands. What on earth was she going to do?

Somewhere a door closed, there was a murmur of voices, Heath's and Bill's, and then firm footsteps crossed the polished wooden floor of the living-room, became muted as they moved along the carpeted hallway. Bree's heartbeats seemed to literally stop as she sat frozen in her bed. She hadn't even locked her door. And if he came in . . . if he touched her, kissed her, she would be lost. The footsteps paused momentarily outside her door and what seemed like a lifetime later moved on past. Bree didn't expel the breath she held locked inside her until the door of his own room shut firmly behind him.

In a frenzy of movement she was out of the bed and across the floor, her fingers finding and fumbling with the coldness of the key in the lock. Her breath came in steadying gulps as the lock clicked solidly closed.

Back in bed she huddled beneath the sheets, shivering with reaction. When Heath returned he would find her totally inaccessible, for it was unlikely that he would break down the door and disturb the Rolands.

In future she would simply have to be strong, keep out of his way as much as possible. And if she could find a job, any job, save enough money to get her a start again she could get away from Heath Durant completely, away from his perturbing presence, his beautiful home, and leave Ben to this better life.

A tiny sharp pain clutched at her. She would miss the baby dreadfully for he was all the family she had now, now that Briony had broken away, but she had to put him first. Here Ben would have a far better chance to make something of his life, far better than she and his mother had had, if she left him to grow up with Heath.

With his own grandfather, she told herself brutally, reminding herself that she must think of Heath only as that, as Ben's grandfather, Reece's father and, as he had said himself, old enough to be her own father. The memory of his hands moving so devastatingly over her body, of his lips plundering hers, made her tense achingly in the comfortable bed. No, never her father. He could never be that.

For what seemed like ages she waited for the sound of his footsteps to return along the hallway, to stop outside her door, for the doorknob to turn, but the sound never came. He had obviously changed his mind, didn't want her as badly as she thought he did, as she had wanted, still wanted him.

Well, it was for the best, she tried to tell herself. She couldn't let him use her. He spoke of wanting, a physical need, but there had been no mention of love. That wasn't in her plan of the way things should be. And afterwards she knew she would have been filled with loathing, completely disgusted with herself. Yes, it was best this way. Even if the ache inside her jeered at her to make the most of this short life in case life passed her by. She crept out of bed and unlocked the door, and eventually, towards dawn, she drifted into a troubled sleep.

'Good morning. lovey. Aren't you a sleepyhead?' smiled Peg as she looked up from wiping the remains of Ben's food from his face as Bree entered the kitchen.

The baby sat in the high-chair Bill had borrowed from their daughter for him, and he gave her his shining baby smile as he waved his spoon in the air and banged it loudly on the high-chair tray. Bree flinched at the jarring sound and crossed to take the spoon from Ben's fingers.

'I'm sorry you were left with feeding Ben, Peg. I must have been dead to the world not to hear him when he woke up. He usually makes such a racket gurgling to himself.'

'You were dead to the world,' Peg teased. 'I peeped in on you nearly an hour ago and I hadn't the heart to wake you up. You were probably tired out, so sit yourself down and relax and I'll fix you some breakfast.' She gave Ben a baby crust to chew on. 'This young man has made short work of his meal, so don't you go worrying about him.' She straightened. 'Now, what you need, Bree, is a big plate of bacon and eggs.'

'Oh, no. No, thanks, Peg. Just a cup of tea and maybe a slice of toast,' Bree assured the older woman hurriedly. 'I'm not very hungry this morning. Really.'

'Tsk! Tsk! I don't know. No wonder you young things are as thin as rakes! You don't eat enough to feed a bird. A puff of wind would knock you over.' Peg shook her head as she slipped a couple of slices of bread into the toaster. 'Lord knows what would happen to you if you were really ill—you'd have nothing to fall back on, that's the truth.'

'I've put on pounds since I came here,' Bree smiled as she looked down at her jeans and top which fitted her properly now and didn't hang on her the way they had done. 'If I'm not careful I'll be growing out of my clothes.'

'I don't think you need to worry about that,' Peg smiled back. 'At least I have to admit that you look a sight better than you did when you came here, all hollow-cheeked and lost-looking.'

'I looked like that?' Bree laughed a little embarrassedly. 'I wasn't that bad, surely?'

'Yes, you were. I was only saying to Heath this morning that these few weeks have done wonders for you.'

At the mention of his name Bree's flush rose and she couldn't raise her eyes from the table as she watched her fingers playing nervously with her cutlery. To think Peg had been discussing her with him too!

'He ... Heath's had his breakfast, then?' she asked unevenly.

'Oh, yes. Not that he ate much either,' Peg added with a frown. 'He brought young Ben along with him, as a matter of fact.'

Bree's eyes flew to Peg in surprise. 'Oh. I hope Ben didn't wake him,' she began.

'I shouldn't think so. Heath's usually up early. I keep telling him it would do him good to have a lie-in occasionally, that he doesn't get enough sleep but,' Peg shrugged, 'there's no telling him.'

'Where is he now? Heath, I mean.' Bree couldn't stop herself asking.

'Heath? Why, he's gone, love. He left a good half hour ago,' Peg told her.

CHAPTER FIVE

'GONE?' Bree could only stare at the other woman.

'Yes. He left straight after breakfast—for the office.' Peg shook her head. 'You'd think it could wait until Monday, wouldn't you? But no, he has to go in today.'

'Oh.' Bree went to take a sip of the tea Peg set down in front of her and then changed her mind when her shaking fingers made the cup rattle in its saucer.

'Didn't you know he was going in to the office either?' Peg asked as she busied herself about the kitchen.

'No. I ... I didn't really ask him,' Bree stammered, still shocked at the catastrophic feeling that had gripped her at the thought of Heath's leaving. In those first few moments her imagination had run riot, thinking he had gone because of her, left on some other business trip as a cover to disguise the fact that he had been irritated by her blatant display of her feelings and wanted time to allow the situation to cool down. She cringed with mortification and tried to tell herself that she was wrong, that he had been as aroused by his emotions as she had been, even if his arousal had been purely physical.

'And he said not to expect him for dinner this evening,' Peg was saying with disapproval as she crossed to the breakfast bar. 'Here's your toast, love.'

The food stuck in Bree's throat, but she

managed to force down one slice of toast before she could make her escape. 'I think I'll take Ben out into the garden for a while before I give him his bath.' She lifted the baby from his high-chair, not looking at Peg, for she knew some of her vulnerable uncertainty was there in her eyes and the older woman's gentle sympathy would be more than she could bear just at this moment.

The remainder of the day passed slowly and now the house without Heath's presence was empty and lonely. And that night, lying awake waiting for his return, Bree tossed about in abject misery. What a fool she'd been! How could she possibly have even considered the idea that a man in Heath's position could ever feel anything lasting for a nonentity like herself? She didn't even know who her parents had been, what they were. Oh, she had their names on her birth certificate, but names without faces meant nothing. When she finally fell into a troubled sleep well into the early hours of the morning she knew Heath still hadn't returned home.

She had almost finished folding some of their washing just before lunch next day when Peg stuck her head around the door.

'Ah, there you are, love.' Peg came into the small airy sewing room which she used for all manner of household activities. It was a pleasant room, the large glass picture window affording a peaceful view of the grounds, the trees and the river.

Bree loved working in here. The room gave her a nice feeling of security and comfort, and with the knowledge that Heath had eventually arrived home and was somewhere in the house adding an anticipatory edge to her already disturbed nervous system she had been more than glad to seek sanctuary in this hideaway.

'Heath wants to see you for a moment.' Peg dropped her unwitting bombshell. 'He's in his study.'

'He wants to see me? What for?' Her voice had thinned in apprehension while her heartbeats raced again.

'I've no idea, but it can't be all that bad, can it?' Peg laughed at the expression on Bree's face. 'Come now, you look like a schoolgirl who's been summoned to the Headmaster's office! Run along—I'll finish that.'

And Bree felt like a schoolgirl too, she grimaced shakily as she walked slowly towards the study. A gauche, naïve, guilty schoolgirl.

The door of the study was closed and Bree stood before it, smoothing the palms of her hands down the side seams of her jeans. Her heartbeats were echoing loudly in her ears as she forced herself to take a deep calming breath before she raised her hand to knock tentatively on the door.

'Come in.' The voice was muffled, but to Bree's supersensitivity it sounded gruff and irritated.

Slowly opening the door, she stepped inside, her knuckles white on the door knob. He didn't look up right away, for he was sitting working at his desk, his hand writing quickly over the page. When he did glance up, his face seemed so devoid of expression that Bree felt her blood chill in her veins. Slowly he laid his pen on the desktop and sat back in his chair, elbows leaning on the armrests, large strong hands clasped loosely together on the desk.

'Come inside, Bree, and close the door,' he said, and when she still hesitated his lips tightened. 'I'm not going to eat you,' he added tersely.

Bree closed the door and stood with eyes downcast, her hands pressed tightly together behind her back, feeling more like an errant schoolgirl with every moment that passed.

'I think we need to talk,' Heath began in an even, unemotional voice and Bree felt the pressure of hot tears behind her eyes. He was going to send them away, she thought dejectedly. 'About the other night,' he added just as indifferently.

'I don't think we need to talk. I'm ...' The words stuck in her throat and she turned away, groping for the door knob.

'Bree, I think we do,' he repeated firmly, his tone stopping her in her tracks. 'Come and sit down. I, at least, have something to say that I feel needs to be said.'

Slowly she turned back to him, sitting on the edge of the chair farthest from him. Heath swore under his breath and pushed himself angrily to his feet in one sharp decisive movement and in a couple of strides he was around the desk.

'For God's sake, I'm not going to pounce on you!' he bit out as she shrank back from him.

He stood towering over her, glaring down, his hands on his hips, his lashes falling to shield the expression in his eyes. His slacks were taut across his muscular thighs and the soft weave of his knit shirt moulded his powerful chest and shoulders, the short sleeves emphasising his developed biceps. He was so tall and arousingly virile standing over her that Bree had to consciously stop herself from reaching out to touch him, wanting to feel the strength of his arms about her again holding her so safely close to him.

Her eyes were on his, slid down to his lips with

unconscious sensuality and she saw his jaw tighten before he turned abruptly away to lean on his hands on the desk, his back to her.

'I suppose I should apologise for my behaviour,' he said flatly. 'I'm not proud of it and it won't happen again.'

Bree stared at his uncompromising back, wishing she could run to him, wrap her arms around him, feel the softness of his shirt beneath her cheek, and she stood up, had taken a couple of tentative steps towards him, only to halt nervously when he swung around to face her again.

'I know it's hardly an excuse, but I was dog-tired that night and I'd been working myself into the ground for weeks. I guess my resistance was at a low.' One corner of his mouth lifted derisively. 'Believe me, I'm not in the habit of taking advantage of young girls.'

'You mean you didn't want to kiss me?' The words were out before she could bite them back and a dull flush washed her face as her eyes fell in embarrassment.

He raised one mocking eyebrow. 'At the time, yes. I can't deny that.'

The tears that hovered behind her eyes gushed forward and she blinked them furiously away, just wanting to run away and hide and somehow ease the pain in her heart. He couldn't be making it more obvious that the whole thing had meant nothing to him.

'But that's beside the point. It shouldn't have happened.' He paused momentarily. 'We both know that, don't we?'

Did they? Bree asked herself torturedly. How could he stand there so self-possessedly and discuss what had been for her the most earth-shattering experience of her life, in such a cold unemotional way?

'Look, Bree, I don't want you to get the wrong impression. That night was a step out of time and won't be repeated,' he said firmly.

Bree looked up at him then and when he saw the unshed tears in her eyes he swore softly again and ran a hand through the thick darkness of his hair.

'Bree, I was tired. I needed a woman—any woman. And you were there,' he said flatly.

'Please, don't ...' She took a gulping breath. 'Don't say any more. I ...'

Heath's hands reached out and clasped her upper arms. 'Bree, I don't go around making love to girls young enough to be my daughter.' A pulse throbbed at the corner of his tense mouth as his eyes roved over her face. 'Especially girls with the glow of innocence written all over them. Although how the hell you manage it when——' He broke off and his fingers tightened on her arms as his eyes seemed to ignite, glowing with a burning heat he was unable to disguise. 'You are my son's——' he paused as a flicker of emotion, anger or pain, crossed his face, 'my son's girl-friend, and as such I had no right to treat you the way I did.' The balls of his thumbs rubbed the skin of her arms with arousing sensuousness, almost as though he couldn't help himself. 'Bree, I ...' His voice broke off, deep with the same passion that shone in the hot blueness of his eyes.

Her body burned with an all-consuming ache, a matching fire, her heart racing with a rapidity that threatened to choke her. His dark head moved downwards and she closed her eyes, not daring to breathe as she waited for the exquisite capturing of her lips by his.

But it never came. He thrust her away from him and strode across the room to stand gazing out through the window, his shoulders moving as he steadied his breathing. Her eyes flew open, could only watch him, and she was suddenly cold, feeling as though part of her had been cruelly severed. She wished her frozen body would move, slink away so she could curl up and die. Even her pride seemed to have vanished.

Gathering herself together, finding some remnants of that elusive self-respect, she lifted her chin. 'Do you want us to leave?' she asked steadily, something dying deep inside her.

He turned back to face her then, his expression cold again. He obviously had himself under control once more.

'No!' His tone brooked no disputation. 'Your place is here with the child.'

Their eyes warred, although Bree knew hers had lost the battle before the skirmish began. However, before either of them could say another word the telephone on the desk pealed stridently, making her jump in fright. Heath reached across and lifted the receiver.

'I've got it, Peg,' he said into the extension. 'Hello, Roslyn.'

Bree stirred uncomfortably, not knowing whether to go or stay, trying not to eavesdrop on the one-sided conversation. But when Heath laughed softly, that same sensual sound that vibrated through her, Bree's eyes went of their own accord to his face. His eyes met hers, held her gaze, appeared to falter momentarily before the cold shutters slipped back in place and he motioned her to wait until he had finished his call.

'Yes, it was a great night,' he smiled into the phone.

Bree's hands were clutched together as she fought not to let him see her pain and misery. Roslyn. Who was she? Had he spent last night with her?

'No, I haven't forgotten.' He glanced at his wristwatch. 'I'll pick you up in about three-quarters of an hour.' He listened again.

'Sure.' He laughed softly, and Bree wondered if that sound had the same effect on the woman on the other end of the telephone line as it had on her. 'See you soon.' He replaced the receiver and looked back at Bree, his jaw set in a hard line.

If he'd wanted to underscore the fact that the other night had been exactly as he'd described it he couldn't have made a better job of it. And she'd thought she could be the special woman in his life! If it didn't hurt so much she would laugh. Heath could have his choice of women. She conjured up a mental picture of the unknown Roslyn. She would be poised, attractive and sophisticated. What could Heath Durant possibly see in someone like Bree Ransome? Her lips tightened to still their tremble.

'Bree——'

'No!' She choked out. 'Don't say anything else. I understand completely.' Her voice was tight and unlike her own, and she turned numbly away.

'Bree!'

She paused with her hand on the doorknob, her back to him, stiffening herself for the pain his words might inflict. She waited like that, but it was tense seconds before he spoke again. She heard his breath expelled in an exasperated sigh.

'I'll be going out now,' was all he said. 'Could you tell Peg I won't be in to lunch.'

After lunch Bree found refuge in the garden,

and she needed to be alone. The strain of pretending everything was all right with her world when she was with Peg made her feel trapped and tense. An hour's pottering about Bill's lovingly tended flower beds brought its own brand of calmness to her.

It was a beautiful day, with clear blue unclouded skies and a soft gentle breeze. Occasional bird calls, the buzz of the cicadas and the faint sound of Bill's rider mower he was working down by the river were the only sounds to disturb the air, and the peacefulness soon began to wash away at least a small portion of Bee's unhappiness.

She had been on the verge of questioning Peg about the woman Roslyn, but each time she had stopped herself, part of her not wanting to know, afraid of what she might hear. It was cowardly, she knew, but the force of her feelings for Heath made it impossible for her to so much as discuss him without some outward sign betraying those feelings.

Perhaps this Roslyn was a relative. Bree paused with her small garden fork dug in the rich earth. His sister? Or a cousin? She grimaced wryly and attacked the soil with renewed vigour. No. Heath's tone of voice had not sounded very cousinly.

Unhappily she decided again she had better make some plan to find work, for without money she was tied here and wouldn't be able to leave with or without Ben. The first step must be to check the Situations Vacant column of the newspaper. Her experience was limited to shop assisting or the factory work of her last job, which she had really hated. She could type. She'd taken a course at night, but unfortunately she'd had no actual typing experience. It was rather like a dog chasing its tail. You couldn't get a job because you had no experience and you couldn't become experienced because no one would give you a job.

So engrossed in the weeding and her own depressing thoughts was she that the approaching car was drawing to a halt in front of the house before she realised it was there. Perhaps Heath—? It wasn't Heath's red Ferrari or the Mercedes but a silver-blue Citroën that squatted on the driveway about ten feet in front of her.

Bree remained where she was on her hands and knees watching the man who climbed from the car and looked at her in surprise.

'Well, hello there! You're a sight for sore eyes.' He smiled as he stepped across the garden strip of purple bachelor's buttons lining the driveway. 'Heath didn't tell me he'd hired more staff.'

The man was of medium height and build, with sandy hair and a fair complexion that wouldn't take easily to the sun, and although he seemed no stranger to the place he was obviously a few years older than Heath.

As Bree stood up slowly the stranger's eyes roamed over her, making her uncomfortably conscious of her faded shorts and revealing tank top.

'I don't work here exactly,' she began. 'I . . . I'm visiting for a while.'

'Visiting?' The sandy eyebrows rose enquiringly. 'Friend of the Rolands', are you?' he asked, his eyes a light hazel colour, still assessing her in a way that she couldn't like.

'No. A friend of Heath's,' she got out breathily.

'I see.' The tone of those two words and the knowing look brought a dull flush to Bree's cheeks, and she sought for some explanation to prove to this man that he saw wrongly.

Was it always going to be like this? What was it that people saw in her that immediately made them think the worst?

'Well then, what say you and I introduce ourselves?' the man smiled, and held out his hand. 'I'm Ranald Hailey, an old friend of Heath's.'

'Bree Ransome.' She slipped off her gardening glove to shake the outstretched hand, pulling her hand firmly away when he held it for far too long.

'Any friend of Heath's is a friend of mine,' he laughed, and she wondered if it was simply her defensive imagination that added a slight pause before the word 'friend'. 'Well, now we know each other, how long have you been here?' Ranald Hailey showed no sign of moving towards the house.

'A couple of weeks,' Bree replied, willing Bill to decide to mow the front lawn of the house. Somehow this Ranald Hailey stood too close to her, his look was too familiar, and quite frankly she didn't like him.

'A couple of weeks!' He frowned. 'I thought Heath was just back from a couple of weeks down south?'

'Yes, he is. He brought me here and then returned to Sydney,' she told him. 'Did you want to see Heath? He's not home at the moment, but perhaps Peg would know where you could reach him. I'll go and ask her.' She made to move towards the house, but he put a hand on her arm to stop her.

'No hurry. This was only a good neighbour visit anyway. I live a couple of kilometres down the road.' He motioned in the direction of the city. 'I didn't have far to come, so Heath's absence doesn't matter at all. Besides, I'd much rather talk to you.'

Bree felt the telltale colour wash her cheeks. 'Thank you.' She accepted the compliment uneasily.

'I never thought to see a young girl blush like that in this day and age,' he said softly. 'I hope Heath realises what a rarity he's got,' he added, a faint almost aggressive emotion momentarily crossing his face.

'Mr Hailey, I think you're under some misapprehension,' Bree began firmly. 'I'm simply a friend of Heath's, nothing more. And I find it quite embarrassing having you imply anything else.'

The light hazel eyes watched her rather sceptically. 'I'm sorry, Bree. May I call you Bree? And you must call me Ranald, or Ran, if you prefer. Well, Bree, I didn't mean to cause any embarrassment. Please accept my apologies if I've offended you.' His smile was all charm and Bree suspected he used that smile as easily as he breathed. 'It's just that Heath—well,' he shrugged, 'let's say he doesn't have any trouble finding friends.'

Those casually spoken words stabbed painfully at Bree and she turned away to lay her gardening gloves on the wheelbarrow to hide the strain that tightened her lips. 'I'm afraid I wouldn't know about that,' she said flatly.

There was a brief pause.

'How long did you say you'd known Heath?'

'I didn't say.' Bree had herself under control again. 'But not long. Not as long as you have, anyway.' She put the ball back in his court,

knowing that was safer, and sensing he'd not be
averse to talking about himself.

'No. I've known Heath for years—more years
than I'll admit to. We met some time before he
married Pamela, actually.' Ranald Hailey's smile
carried a knowing, almost mocking edge to it.
'Pamela and I were school friends, and Heath
worked for her father, you know.'

'Oh.' Bree's curiosity was aroused. She wished
she could pretend it wasn't, but she had to admit
that she wanted to know everything there was to
know about this man who had the power to uplift
or crush her.

'Yes,' continued the other man. 'He took over
old Jack Andrews' business when the old man
retired through ill-health. Heath started out
apprenticed to Jack and—well, by then he'd
married the boss's daughter and stepped in when
his father-in-law stepped out.'

Although this was said with a laugh Bree heard
the underlying reproach. Reading between Ranald
Hailey's lines, the implication was that Heath had
married the daughter and come up with the
company.

'The business seems to be doing very well,' Bree
ventured, not knowing what else to say, her mind
trying to assimilate all that Ranald Hailey was
saying and was leaving unsaid.

Ranald Hailey nodded grudgingly. 'Andrews'
wasn't the concern it is today when Heath took the
reins, I'll grant Heath that. It's now Durant
Enterprises, among other things, and a multi-
million dollar set-up. Unfortunately old Jack never
lived to see it. He died not long after he retired.'

'Pamela was his only child, then?' probed Bree.

'Mmm.' He looked a little reflective and a frown

formed two furrows between his eyebrows.
'Pamela was the only one. Spoiled, of course, but a
beautiful spoiled goddess,' he finished softly. 'One
of the most beautiful women I've ever seen.' His
lips twisted bitterly before he gave a harsh laugh.
'The talk of the town, I suppose you'd say.' He
seemed to find that even more coldly amusing.

'What happened to her?' Bree couldn't stop
herself asking, although she despised herself for
doing it.

'She . . .' He stopped and glanced sharply at her.
'Pamela was a very unhappy lady. Maybe she died
of unhappiness.' He turned and walked back
towards his car, leaving Bree to stare after him.

He stopped by the driver's side door, his hand
on the door handle and turned back to her. 'I'd
best be off.' His eyes were moving over her again
with a brooding concentration that was somehow
worse than his previous lecherousness, for it struck
a chill inside Bree making her shiver with an
unwarranted foreboding.

'Tell Heath I said hello.'

Before Bree could reply Heath's red Ferrari pulled
to a halt in front of the garage and they both turned
towards it, watching the tall muscular figure climb
from behind the wheel and pause momentarily, his
eyes taking in the man by the silver-blue Citroën and
then moving to Bree as she remained by the
wheelbarrow, somehow unable to move. The door
of the Ferrari closed with a restrained click and then
long lithe strides ate up the space between them.

He was wearing the same thigh-hugging dark
blue slacks and short sleeved white knit shirt that
he'd worn this morning in his study. Was it only
mere hours ago? Bree asked herself incredulously.
It seemed like another life away. The sun shone on

the dark sheen of his hair as the breeze lifted it gently back from his face. A live black panther couldn't have looked as sleekly smooth, as vitally alive, as potentially dangerous as Heath Durant did as he approached them with seemingly deliberately measured strides.

'Heath! Almost missed you,' Ranald Hailey said jovially, his good humour revived, and slapped Heath on the back with the air of an old and valued friend.

'To what do we owe the pleasure of your visit, Ran?' Heath asked him evenly enough, although his expression was hardly welcoming.

'Nothing in particular,' replied the other man. 'I heard you were back, so I drove over to see how things went down south.'

'They went well.' Heath was noncommittal.

'Good, good. Nothing like a personal appearance to put things right.'

'Things weren't all that wrong.' Heath leant back against the Citroën and folded his arms. 'I think your information source has been giving you a bum steer again.'

'You know me, Heath. I rarely take gossip with more than a grain of salt,' laughed Ran.

Heath's eyes held his for some seconds before his gaze slanted across to look at Bree, and she hastily reached for her gardening gloves, disconcerted that he most probably thought she was eavesdropping. She neither wanted to be part of the conversation nor wanted his eyes to be on her for fear she inadvertently gave herself away.

'I've just been introducing myself to Bree.' Ranald's eyes had followed Heath's and had narrowed speculatively. 'She tells me she's a friend of yours.'

'Yes,' Heath affirmed eventually, while the tension that emanated from him filled the clear afternoon air.

'We had an interesting conversation, didn't we, Bree?' His light hazel eyes were sharply alert to Heath's expression.

Ranald Hailey was like a snake, Bree thought as she watched the two men, a snake that enticed, manipulated, before the strike. And there was no love lost here, no matter how lasting a friendship Ranald Hailey professed there was between the two men. There was no mistaking the restrained antagonism in every taut line of Heath's body.

'We weren't talking for very long,' Bree said uneasily as her eyes met Heath's and veered away.

'Well, maybe I lost track of the time,' laughed Ranald loudly. 'Your fresh young beauty be-dazzled me. She is bedazzling, isn't she, Heath?' He turned to the other man. 'A breath of fresh air to a couple of old campaigners like us, don't you think?'

'If I listened to you, Ran, I'd be reaching for my walking stick,' Heath remarked drily.

'We can still go a few rounds, can't we?' Ranald laughed again, and the sound began to jar and set Bree's teeth on edge.

The screen door banged closed and the three of them turned as Peg approached carrying Ben in her arms.

'You're back, Heath!' she beamed, and as she turned to face the other man her smile faded just a little. 'Hello, Mr Hailey. I didn't know we had visitors.'

'I thought I was more than a visitor, Peg, almost part of the family,' Ranald teased, and Peg made no reply to his statement.

'I've a cup of tea made, if anyone would like one. I was just coming out to see if Bree wanted to take a break.'

'Love one, Peg,' Ranald accepted immediately. 'No one makes tea like you do. And I'm sure Bree's ready for one, working out here in the sun.' His eyes went to the baby. 'But this is a surprise, Peg.' He indicated Ben. 'When did your little stranger arrive? I must say you kept it very hush-hush!'

Peg's lips thinned and, embarrassed for her, Bree hurried forward to take the baby from her. 'I didn't realise he was awake, Peg. He hasn't been a nuisance, has he?'

'Of course not, the little pet.' Her face softened. 'Would you like your tea out here on the patio, Heath?'

'Thanks, Peg.' Heath smiled faintly at her.

'Right. Sit yourselves down and I'll bring out the tray.' She disappeared inside and they walked up the steps to the patio set on the verandah.

Heath motioned Bree into the chair he held out for her before sitting himself down opposite her and leaning back in his chair, his long legs stretched out in front of him, his eyes finding some interest in the highly polished toes of his handmade leather shoes.

An uncomfortable silence lay between them as they waited for Peg's return. Bree untangled Ben's fingers from her hair, feeling Ranald Hailey's eyes on her with a smiling mockery he barely made an attempt to hide.

'Cute little fellow,' he remarked. 'Just like his mother.' His smile was becoming as irritating to Bree as his laugh.

'He does take after my side of the family,' she

said carefully, wishing she possessed the command to tell him straight out that he had it all wrong, that Heath was not the baby's father. She knew Briony wouldn't have so much as hesitated. Briony would have taken it in her stride. But with her cheeks burning, it was beyond Bree just at that moment.

'Here we are!' Peg's return broke the tension. She set the tray on the table and began to pour the tea. 'Did you have a nice lunch, Heath?' she asked.

'Yes, thanks, Peg.' Heath took a sip of his tea and smiled at Peg before she left them to return to the kitchen.

Bree lifted her own cup, only to have Ben make a lunge for it, and she set the hot liquid hurriedly back on the table. Calmly Heath reached across and took the baby from her with a naturalness that brought a flush to her cheeks.

'I'll hold him. Drink your tea,' he said, and Ranald Hailey's eyebrows rose towards his receding hairline.

'Aren't you domesticated?' he remarked. 'Seems you haven't lost your touch.'

'Seems so.' Heath replied, undaunted.

'Which reminds me—any word on Reece?' the other man asked casually.

There was a heavy pause and Bree's eyes went involuntarily to meet Heath's, and a moment before the thick lashes shielded their blueness a heart-stopping flare of emotion sent Bree's heart rate skyrocketing. She couldn't begin to understand that play of emotions, but the flash of pain was as obvious as the reason behind it was obscure.

'Nothing concrete.' Heath said flatly.

'Tsh! Young scoundrel,' muttered Ranald, and

the conversation floundered somewhat as they all seemed captured by their own thoughts.

'I suppose I should be off.' Ranald set his cup on its saucer. 'I've a few other calls to make. No doubt I'll see you at the party on Tuesday night?' he directed at Heath as he stood up.

Heath stood, too, and shrugged. 'I suppose so. It's in aid of a good cause.'

'Aren't all of the lady's parties in aid of a good cause?' Ranald paused and turned his eyes on Bree and they flickered with sudden brightness. 'Are you going, Bree?'

Bree shook her head. 'No.'

'Pity. You'd have enjoyed it—give you a chance to meet everyone.' He shot a glance at Heath. 'If you're going straight to the party from the office, Heath, I'd be happy to collect Bree and bring her along.'

'Oh, no, I ...' Bree began hurriedly, not wanting to go anywhere with Ranald Hailey, knowing instinctively that his offer was made more as a jibe at Heath than a courtesy, and the feeling that long-running deep-seated hostilities lurked just below the surface with the two men was more blatantly apparent than ever.

'Thanks, Ran, but sorry,' Heath's words ran over Bree's. 'I just didn't get time to mention the party to Bree. But she will be going.' His face was stonily cold. 'She'll be going with me.'

CHAPTER SIX

'I CAN'T possibly go to any party!' A couple of hours had passed since the departure of their visitor, and Bree stood facing Heath across his study once more.

As Ranald Hailey's car had disappeared down the driveway Heath had handed the baby back to Bree and withdrawn to his study before she could find her voice. Her shock at his statement had fleetingly robbed her of speech.

Now Ben had been fed and tucked into his cot and Peg had disclaimed the need for her help with the preparations for their evening meal, so Bree had come timorously in search of Heath to sort out the situation of the party.

Heath's eyes watched her coldly, his fingers irritatedly shuffling his papers as though he had no time to spare for trivial interruptions.

'To any party, or to any party with me?' he ground out with a dark frown.

'That's not what I meant.' Bree raised her hands and let them fall to her sides. What would he say if she told him she'd go anywhere, to hell and back, if only she was going with him? 'I meant I can't go to any parties. I have Ben to look after.'

'Peg would be more than willing to babysit.' He pushed that aside. 'Besides, the baby will be fast asleep before we leave. The party won't begin to get under way until eight o'clock at the earliest. Which will give me adequate time to come home, shower and change so we can be off before a quarter to eight.'

'I can't go—I'm sorry.'

He stood up and walked slowly around the desk to stand in front of her, and Bree valiantly quelled the urge to back away, keep as much distance as possible between them. For her own safety.

'Can't or don't want to?' His finger lifted her chin.

'Can't,' she all but whispered as his nearness began to have its usual overwhelming effect on her.

'Why? I'll need more reasons than having to leave the baby with Peg,' he added firmly.

'I don't have——' she took a steadying breath, 'I haven't anything with me that would be suitable to wear to a party,' she admitted reluctantly.

'I see.' He watched her carefully, as though he was trying to see inside her. 'You haven't a thing to wear?' he grimaced.

'I haven't. You can look in my wardrobe if you don't believe me,' she said defiantly.

'Where are your party clothes?' he asked, and her eyes couldn't hold his.

'I . . . Please, Heath. I just don't want to go to the party,' she told him softly.

She felt his eyes move over her face, and her nerve ends tingled as though he was physically caressing her.

'I want you to come,' he said evenly.

'I won't know anyone there, and I'm really not fond of parties.'

'Then you must have been at loggerheads with Reece quite often. He seemed to thrive on them.' He turned away and walked back to his desk to slide a cigarette from the packet on the desktop.

'Tomorrow morning you can come into the city with me,' he flicked the lighter to the end of his cigarette and exhaled slowly, 'and you can get something to wear to the party.'

'I can't do that!' Bree burst out, ignoring his reference to Reece.

Heath sighed with evident exasperation. 'You can and you will,' he said calmly. 'It doesn't have to be too formal. It won't be that sort of party.'

'I'm sorry, I don't have the money to spend on clothes I'm only going to wear once in a blue moon.'

'I thought every female craved a new party dress,' he said lightly.

'Well, I can't afford that luxury.' Her anger began to bubble. 'It may be fine for all your rich friends to saunter into exclusive boutiques and buy whatever takes their fancy and to hell with the cost, but some of us can't do that, Mr Durant. I'm afraid I'm not in your class. I have to count every cent I spend, and I'm not wasting what little money I have on the type of outfit that would be acceptable to your friends. I could be out fending for myself again at any time, and I don't want to be left without money to feed myself and Ben, let alone keep a roof over our heads.' Her voice died away as she suddenly realised what she was saying.

A heavy silence filled the room and her whole body seemed to go cold. Apprehensively she raised her eyes to look across at Heath, expecting a blazing anger, but his expression was as impassive as ever as he regarded her through a faint smoky haze.

'I'm sorry,' she muttered. 'I shouldn't have said that. I was angry.'

'I didn't expect you to pay for the dress

yourself,' he said evenly. 'A friend of mine has a
dress shop, near my office. You can go there and
buy whatever you need.'

'I can't take your money!' Bree was horrified.

The air became thicker and his stance took on a
portentous tension.

'It's not that I'm not grateful for your offer,' she
hurried to add. 'But the fact that you're letting us,
Ben and me, stay here in your house, is more than
enough in itself, so I can't let you—well ... It's
not as though I'm anything to you.' Bree felt
herself flush, realising that her last statement had a
double meaning.

'Consider it as wages,' he said, 'for services
rendered.'

Bree's face paled. Surely he didn't mean——?
He couldn't be so cruel!

'For your work in the garden, for helping Peg.'
He frowned again. 'And about that, Bree. It's not
necessary, you know. I don't want you working
yourself into the ground so that you feel you're
paying your way.'

'I like helping Peg and I enjoy doing the garden
with Bill,' she told him honestly.

'You're my guest, Bree. As long as you don't
forget that,' Heath said quietly, and picked up a
sheaf of papers. 'Be ready at eight in the morning.'
His tone was dismissing and she could only turn
and leave him, knowing he didn't intend that there
be any further discussion.

The drive into Brisbane next morning was slightly
unreal to Bree, and as she watched the passing
green paddocks beginning to merge into the more
closely settled suburbs she couldn't help but
wonder if she could be dreaming it all. Had

anyone told her a little over a month ago, as she sat in her dingy room in Bundaberg with no job, little money and the prospect of finding somewhere else to live, that she would be reclining in the comfortably luxurious confines of a red Ferrari beside the most attractive, most compelling man she could ever have imagined, she would have been the first to laugh in disbelief.

Slanting a sideways glance at him, she felt her heart quicken with the wonder, the amazement of it all. His chiselled profile was so achingly familiar that she felt deep down that she had known him all her life, and so much longer, perhaps in some previous existence.

His strong hands moved to change gear and the powerful car surged forward with the refined throb of a thoroughbred as he dexterously changed lanes and they made a brief run along the river before the convergence of traffic slowed them down again.

'Times like these, there's a lot to be said in support of a helicopter,' Heath remarked wryly as they stopped at a red traffic light.

'Yes, it would be faster,' Bree agreed softly, wishing she could make bright interesting conversation instead of suffering in inadequate silence.

No wonder he found her wanting! She couldn't hope to compare favourably with the jet-setting women in his circle. Somehow she suspected she was going to be rather like a fish out of water at this party. How she wished he could see and understand that, and not insist that she accompanied him! She sighed unconsciously, and Heath turned to glance at her.

'Unfortunately the traffic's always thick this time of morning. A city workers' hazard.'

'Oh, that's all right. I mean, I don't mind,' she stuttered into an embarrassed quiet again, feeling even more miserable than she had before.

The lights flashed to green and the snake of cars crawled on towards the grouping of high-rise buildings that marked the city.

Heath's office was in a multi-storied block just out of the main city centre, and he drove the Ferrari into the under street level car park. Climbing out of the car, he handed the keys to the young attendant, who flew across towards him beaming a welcoming 'good morning'. Heath held Bree's door open and helped her out of her seat, and the young man gave her an open look of admiration tinged faintly with curiosity.

'Just park it, Glenn,' Heath told him. 'Don't race it.'

'Sure, Mr Durant. You know me,' the young man grinned broadly, his eyes moving appreciatively over Bree once more, his smile widening.

She automatically smiled back at him, and then Heath's hand had firmly taken her arm and he was striding across to the elevators at a pace that had her almost running to keep up with him. Inside the lift he fixed his eyes in front of him, his expression set, and as she stood soundlessly beside him she could feel his incomprehensible anger, a tight band of pain clutching at her.

What could have upset him? What could she possibly have done? She swallowed nervously and her throat closed, causing her to smother a cough. He turned to look at her then, his eyes dark and stormy, but anything he was about to say was interrupted by the opening of the lift doors. Without commenting he motioned for her to precede him into what was obviously the street level foyer.

A couple of people were passing through, moving around the reception desk, and one or two were waiting for the elevator. They afforded Heath and Bree cursory glances which turned into stares of surprises as they recognised their boss and took in the figure of the young woman beside him.

Their attention brought a wash of colour to Bree's face, but Heath barely acknowledged their hasty greetings as he led her through the electronically operated front doors and out on to the pavement.

'The boutique is called 'Jacqui's', and it's straight down to the corner and around to your left, three doors along,' he said clippedly, then his eyes touched on Bree for a moment and some of her uncertainty must have been visible on her face, because he sighed and the harshness of his features relaxed.

'I've phoned ahead to tell them to expect you, so just go along and choose whatever you want,' he said a little less severely. 'And when you've finished come back here and I'll have someone drive you home.'

Bree stood beside him, wanting to beg him to come along with her, but she knew he couldn't and more probably wouldn't and her eyes fell dejectedly. His hands went to her shoulders, turning her around, giving her a gentle push in the right direction. She took a couple of steps and turned back to face him, but he held up his hand before she could speak.

'No more about not wanting any clothes. I insist.' He smiled then, the smile that vibrated through her, turned her legs to water, and a lump rose in her throat.

She loved him so much that just his smile hurt. But it was such an exquisite, nerve-toning pain. Yes, she loved him. As sure as the warm morning sun shone down on her she knew she was head over heels, and just as suddenly the first cloud dulled the sunshine inside her. Heath must never know how deeply she had fallen, for if she embarrassed him further with her feelings he would surely send her away. She used all her willpower to keep the telltale emotion from her face.

'See you later.' He went to turn away.

'Heath!' Her voice stopped him and he swung back. 'What . . . Who do I ask for when I get to the boutique?'

There was a pause before he replied.

'Roslyn Jacobs,' he said casually as the doors slid open, and then his long strides carried him inside. The soundless closing of the doors after him couldn't have told Bree more plainly that he was out of her reach, she was on the outside.

The rack of clothes grew larger and Bree stared incredulously at the array of colours. There was no denying the fact that each outfit was beautiful, that the clothes chosen by this arrestingly attractive, impeccably groomed woman could have been designed exclusively for Bree, and her five foot six inches of height and nicely curved body did do justice to the slacks and tops and the fashionable length dresses that she seemed to have been climbing in and out of for hours. But she'd just have to stop it all right here.

'Please—I can't take all these,' she began.

'Nonsense!' Roslyn Jacobs brushed her words aside and motioned to a young assistant to begin carefully parcelling up the outfits. 'I have strict instructions from Heath.'

Besides the slacks and tops and the dresses there were matching accessories and even a microscopic brown and cream bikini and a beach jacket.

Roslyn flicked quickly through the rack and pulled out a light blue suit. 'I think you should wear this now.' She passed the outfit to Bree and picked up the inexpensive cotton skirt and blouse that Bree had worn into the shop with a barely disguised expression of distaste and put them with the other clothes to be wrapped.

Before Bree could protest she was being helped into a pale blue top of light loose-knit cotton which moulded her full shape, its low neckline skimming the rising mounds of her breasts. A skirt of a darker shade of blue in a lightweight material was slipped over her head, the cut of the skirt hugging her hips to fall swirling about her legs as she stepped across to take the matching short-sleeved jacket from the other woman.

'And these shoes.' Bree's sandals disappeared and the shoes and a pair of stockings were put into Bree's hands.

The pile of gaily wrapped packages began to grow, and as Bree stepped into the shoes she stared at it aghast. 'I won't be able to take all of them today,' she said softly, a worried frown on her brow.

'Have you any make-up?' Roslyn gazed critically at Bree's face.

'Yes. In . . . in my bag.' She picked up her small denim carryall and Roslyn reached across to the counter.

'Put everything into this,' she gave Bree a tooled leather handbag that matched her shoes.

Nervous under the other woman's critical scrutiny Bree applied a little make-up and brushed out her slightly dishevelled hair. She had to admit that the blue of the suit added a bright smoky reflection to her grey eyes, and her long fair hair shone as it fell in a thick sheath down her back.

'We'll be sending these out this afternoon.' Roslyn picked up a small docketbook and the gold pen in her scarlet-tipped fingers hovered over the page. 'Bree Ransome, wasn't it? And what address?'

'Oh.' Bree did a double-take and warm colour flooded her cheeks. 'I'm afraid I don't know the exact address. I'm staying with Heath, with Mr Durant.'

The pen stilled and Roslyn Jacob's cold dark eyes seemed to chill into chipped ice. 'You're staying with Heath?' she asked. 'I was under the impression that you were the friend of a friend of his.'

'Yes—well, I guess I am,' she stammered. 'He ... Heath was kind enough to ... to ask me to stay for a while.'

Bree found it hard to meet those sharp, expertly made up eyes that she knew instinctively hadn't missed her heightened colour.

It was, after all, highly unlikely that the woman Heath had spoken to on the telephone was not this sophisticated creature. Roslyn wasn't a common name and somehow Bree sensed that this was the type of woman that would be able to meet a man like Heath Durant on his own level. Tall and slender, with slightly slanting dark eyes and deep black hair pulled back in a style that should have been too severe for her face but only seemed to draw more attention to her mysterious beauty,

Roslyn Jacobs was exactly the kind of women to catch the eye of Heath Durant. Bree couldn't guess at her age, but she suspected the other woman was at least ten years older than herself. And a lifetime older in experience, she thought ruefully.

'I see.' The words were dripped icicles as Roslyn's pen scrawled on the docket book. 'You're a friend of a friend of Heath's?' she persisted.

'That's right.' Well, it wasn't exactly untrue, Bree tried to tell herself. 'We met in Sydney.' Why had she said that? She shrank inside. She just wasn't cut out to carry this type of half deception, especially with this woman whose sharp eyes missed nothing and who was also thinking the worst, if her expression was anything to go by.

'How long will you be staying?' Roslyn asked.

'I'm not sure,' Bree shrugged, colouring again. 'I guess I should be going. I'd like to have a look around the city before I go home ... back to He ... Mr Durant's.'

She turned away. She had to get out of the shop, away from those razor-edged disapproving eyes, and the anger the other woman was barely disguising as it reached out to almost physically touch her.

'Thank you—for your help with the clothes,' Bree mouthed as she almost ran out into the sunshine, the clear air, taking the opposite direction to Heath's office, needing to put a distance between both Heath and Roslyn Jacobs.

Browsing past the gaily arrayed shop windows, Bree knew only part of her attention was on the displayed merchandise. Try as she might, she couldn't get Heath and Roslyn out of her thoughts, and the most upsetting thing about it all was the fact that she had to admit that Roslyn

Jacobs might have some basis for her grievance. After all, hadn't Heath himself given her the impression that they were more than just friends? The tone of his voice on the telephone had made that plain.

Bree stopped and gazed sightlessly at an assortment of crockery. It must have come as an unpleasant shock to Roslyn when she learned that Bree was staying with Heath, no matter how innocent the situation was. Innocent? That was a laugh! Bree grimaced at her face reflected in the plate glass window. The whole situation was becoming more sordid by the minute.

She sighed again and her eyes moved downwards over her figure, a translucent reflection in the shop window, and she barely suppressed a start of surprise at the transformation. The blue suit certainly did more for her than the much-laundered skirt and blouse had done.

A tiny smile lifted the corners of her mouth. Would Heath . . .? No! She mustn't even think things like that. Heath Durant was nothing to her. She had to make sure she remembered that.

Dipping into the precious cache of her money, she bought herself some new underwear, not nearly as expensive or exclusive as the clothes she had chosen for her at the boutique, but in a small way it helped to salve her pride. And then she had nothing to keep her from returning to his office. As she approached the doors her knees felt like rubber and her heart began to race erratically. Taking a deep steadying breath, she stepped cautiously into the path of the electronic eye, and the doors slid mockingly open.

The girl at the reception desk directed her to the fifteenth floor, and Bree walked slowly across to the elevator that stood ready with its doors open. Stepping inside, she pushed the right button and the lift doors closed on her. Bree shivered. All these silently flowing doors made you feel as though you were trapped, caught in a concrete and steel web. And that seemed suddenly fitting, for she knew she was caught and tied in the bonds of her love for Heath Durant. Come into my parlour, said the spider to the fly. Bree's mouth twisted in a self-derisive smile, knowing she was stepping inside of her own free will, when she knew she should be running away for her own emotional survival, knowing that the spider awaited her coming.

Heath's secretary was a pleasant middle-aged woman with short greying hair and dark-rimmed glasses, and she showed not a flicker of surprise or curiosity as she rang through to tell Heath that Bree was there.

'Go on in, Miss Ransome,' she said with a smile, indicating the door by her desk, and then continued her typing.

The palms of Bree's hands were damp as she knocked lightly and turned the doorknob, stepping nervously inside and closing the door after her. Her eyes widened in amazement, for the room was the most spacious and luxurious office she had seen in her life.

The high heels of her new shoes seemed to sink into the deep pile carpet and her eyes went from the two arresting landscape oils on the pale walls to the huge desk that was a sea of paperwork. Heath frowned over a typed sheet in his hand, and as her eyes rested on him she wished she could obey the dictates of her heart and fly across to wrap her arms around him and soothe away the frown that furrowed his brow. But she stood her ground, her fingers playing with the plaited leather strap of her handbag.

He had shed his jacket and his dark hair fell forward as though he had run his hands through it, and he had pulled loose the knot of his tie and undone the top button on his cream shirt.

'Won't be a moment, Bree,' he said absently, and his eyes rose to glance at her, went down to the papers in his hand, and just as quickly came back to Bree.

His eyes narrowed as they ran over her and she swallowed nervously, her heartbeats accelerating, wishing she could get some inkling of his thoughts from his expression—but of course she couldn't. He was as enigmatic as ever.

'I don't mind waiting if you're busy,' she managed.

He nodded slowly. 'Take a seat.' He motioned to one of the easy chairs by the large plate glass window that made up almost the entire wall. A light open-weave curtain cut out the glare but let plenty of natural light into the office, and instead of sitting down Bree stood with her back to him in front of the window, taking in the view.

At any other time she would have appreciated and been impressed by the panorama of the Brisbane River and the Riverside Expressway and bridge, but she was far too conscious of the man behind her, her hearing supertuned to each movement he made, the shuffle of his papers, the scratch of his pen. The quiet creak of his chair when he eventually stood up and crossed the carpet to stand by her had her senses rising to screaming pitch.

'If that outfit is any indication of the success of your morning, I heartily approve,' he said softly, the deep huskiness of his voice sending a tantalising tingle along her backbone.

She turned slightly, to find he was far too close to her, and she murmured a breathy 'thank you'.

'I'm afraid there was too much for me to carry with me,' she began, 'so Miss ... Miss Jacobs was going to send it out.' She swallowed quickly. 'Heath, there were far too many things, but Miss Jacobs insisted and—well, we'll have to send it back,' she finished in a rush.

'I'm sure Roslyn only carried out my instructions,' he said easily.

'But the cost ...' She stopped as he frowned.

'There's no fear that it will bankrupt me, Bree,' he said drily.

'But it was only to be one dress for the party, and it turned out to be a whole wardrobe of clothes,' she told him guiltily.

'Don't you like them?' His eyes moved over her fair hair, backlit and highlighted by the sunlight through the window.

'Of course I do! Who wouldn't? I've never seen clothes like them in my life, outside of fashion magazines,' she replied honestly. 'But you must see that I can't accept so much.'

Heath shoved his hands into his pockets and the material of his trousers strained across his thighs. 'Would it make you feel any better if I asked you to accept the clothes from me on behalf of my son?' he asked flatly, and her eyes went to his face, trying desperately to read his closed expression.

'Reece would never buy me things like that,' she said, the mention of Reece only adding to her guilt. Reece rarely bought her sister anything, let alone herself. Beside, Reece always spurned what he called the capitalistic rip-offs of the whole structure of the commercial industries.

Heath's lips thinned. 'I guess he wouldn't at that.' He gazed at her speculatively. 'I wonder what he would buy with that kind of money?'

'He . . . I know he wanted a new motorbike,' she put in tentatively, speaking almost to herself.

His eyes rested on her broodingly, began to play over her face, touched her eyes, teased her lips, and she shivered, feeling the tension charged air that began to envelop them. Slowly Heath reached out and lifted her left hand, feeling her ringless finger. 'A motorbike? But no wedding ring,' he sneered.

Snatching her hand away, Bree hurried blindly for the door. She couldn't stay a moment longer, couldn't bear his derision, not while the almost irresistible pull of his magnetism drew her unbearably closer to him with painful inevitability. And if she did stay she knew she could quite easily blurt out the truth, and what small part she had of Heath Durant she would lose. For suddenly that small part of him, just being near him, became infinitely precious to her, something she couldn't bear to surrender so soon.

Her fingers had almost reached the doorknob when his hands gripped her shoulders from behind, stopping her reckless flight, holding her motionless.

CHAPTER SEVEN

NEITHER of them spoke as they stood like that, Bree with her back to him, her heart pounding, not capable of moving as his fingers tightened on her shoulders. The small gaping space between them screamed loudly to be filled with the mergence of their bodies.

Slowly Heath propelled her backwards until she was against him, her body moulded to the hard masculine contours of him, her nerve ends alive and quivering, rising in a deafening tumult of awareness.

His breath stirred the silky fairness of her hair and his lips nuzzled her sensitive earlobe as his hands slid from her shoulders, his arms crossing to hold her to him, his hands spread over the flatness of her midriff beneath her jacket. And she burned where he touched her.

Gently caressing, his lips followed the line of her neck and Bree shivered, moving unconsciously against him, exulting in his obvious response. She heard him catch his breath and his arms tightened about her, his hands sliding upwards to cup her full breasts, easily finding her hardening nipples.

A low moan began way down in her throat, escaping on a deep husky note, a sensually alluring sound she scarcely recognised as her own, and Heath turned her around in the circle of his arms, his lips lowering to possess hers with a passion she matched without reservation.

They were hungry for each other, as though

their bodies had been craving for the touch of each other since the night they had been interrupted by Peg's and Bill's return. Bree's back was against the door, her body trapped by the heady weight of Heath's against her, capturing her. But it was such an effortless seizure, for she made not even a token protest. Heath only had to touch her and she melted against him, totally his, with no thought of denial.

His lips surrendered hers, and they were both breathless, as though they had been running long-distance, and still breathing heavily, he rained light kisses on her eyelids, the tip of her nose, before claiming her pliant mouth once more. His eyes were a fiery glow, the deep purple-blue of the ocean, and she was slowly but surely drowning in them, being drawn in, knowing where he was luring her but unashamedly and unconditionally allowing herself to be led.

The thin cotton knit of her new shirt was a hindrance, and his hands slid beneath it, upwards to cover her lace-encased breasts so that she strained against him, her lips nibbling sensually along the length of his jawline. The pressure of his hard thighs burned through the material of her skirt, one long leg insinuating itself between hers, igniting her, driving all conscious thought from her mind.

Now her mind contained only thoughts of Heath, of the intensely sensuous demands he was making of her body, demands she was meeting, and of the needs within her that he was so easily arousing.

They were lost in each other, moving in a world of their own making, their senses lifting them on to a higher plane. The luxury of Heath's office had faded and the sound of the intercom went unnoticed for some seconds, before Bree realised that Heath's body was still, that the caressing movements of hands had ceased and the noise was not a buzzing in her ears.

Heath swore softly and keeping one arm firmly around her moved with her across towards his desk, half sitting on the top. As he leaned over to flick the switch on the intercom he pulled Bree against him so that she was still encircled by his arm, her body between his long legs, close against him, her hands resting on the breadth of his chest, fingers sliding over his skin as she undid the top buttons of his shirt.

His hand was beneath her blouse, played over her backbone, as his secretary's voice apologetically filled the room.

'I'm sorry to bother you, Heath, but King Martelli's on the line from Ipswich and he insists it's important.'

Heath sighed, his fingers gently caressing her skin. 'Okay, Jill. Give me a minute and then put him through.' His eyes ran over Bree's face and his fingers moved up to slide into the softness of her hair, holding her head at just the right angle for her mouth to accept the gentle kiss he placed on her still swollen lips.

'You'd better tidy up,' he said huskily, his eyes roving over her as though he couldn't stop himself and her nerve ends vibrated in response. 'Or else everyone will know for sure that I've just made love to you instead of simply suspecting I have!' He gave her a crooked grin. 'There's a washroom through there,' he motioned to an unobtrusive door to one side of the office. As Bree walked unsteadily across to do as he directed his phone rang and he picked it up.

'King—what's the trouble?'

He'd already forgotten her. Bree felt a cold pain clutch at her heart. Only a split second ago he had been lost in an earth-shattering passion. And he had been aroused; she could not have been mistaken about it. But now that was behind him and he was once again the self-possessed business-man in dispassionate command of himself.

Bree paused at the door of the bathroom and turned to look at him, her heart aching. But his eyes were still following her, devouring her, and the fire burned just as strongly, frightening her with its intensity, more so because she had expected uninterest, and she stumbled into the bathroom, closing the door between them as she fought for the breath that was trapped in her throat. She'd been wrong; he hadn't forgotten her.

'Bree.' He knocked on the door and swung it open.

She had smoothed her clothes and renewed her make-up with a shaking hand. As she drew her brush through her hair she turned towards him, colour washing her cheeks.

He had rebuttoned his shirt and straightened his tie and his eyes moved over her, their expression now shielded by his half closed lids.

'Ready?' he asked easily.

She nodded and stepped unsteadily towards him, afraid of his nearness, but he had moved away to lift his suit jacket from his chair and shrugged his arms into the sleeves.

Watching him, she felt that same rush of physical awareness, of wanting to reach out and touch him, and she swallowed tensely. Was he going to take her home himself? But he was so obviously busy.

'I can get a taxi back,' she said softly. 'You don't have to leave . . . leave everything.'

Heath paused in the act of running a comb through his thick hair and then began to collect together the papers on his desk, slipping them into his briefcase. 'All this looks worse than it is,' he half smiled, glancing across at her as he snapped the case closed.

'Heath, I . . .' Her voice faded and her gaze fell to her hands. 'I don't mind if you get someone else to run me home. I don't want to interrupt your work.' She glanced up. 'Maybe the young man in the car park could . . .' She didn't finish the sentence.

'No!' he overrode her sharply, his face suddenly icily angry.

'All right,' Bree murmured uncertainly. 'I just don't want to be any trouble.'

His lips twisted self-derisively. 'Trouble!' he breathed to himself. 'Trouble!' He gave a harsh laugh and his hands reached out, pulling her roughly against him, his lips swooping on to hers, punishing her, forcing her head backwards until she felt faint, her hands pushing ineffectually against his chest.

Just as suddenly as it had begun the painful crush of his arms relaxed, the violation of her lips, became a sensual caress, and Bree half collapsed against him. When his lips left hers he sighed agonisedly, his hands behind her head holding her face to his chest, the heavy thud of his heartbeat against her cheek.

'No more talk of trouble,' he said flatly, his breath stirring her hair. 'Do you want to go straight home now?' he asked, holding her away from him, his eyes as bleak as an overcast sky.

'Not particularly,' she said, just wanting to be with him. 'I don't want to be in the way, but if I have a choice I'll stay,' she added quickly, her colour rising again.

Heath dragged his eyes from the tremble of her lips. 'If we stay here you know what will happen,' he said softly, his finger reaching out to slowly follow the low edge of her neckline, pausing to rest in the valley between her breasts.

Her eyes were mesmerised by his and the air between them seemed to spark with electricity. All trace of Heath's anger had gone and a pulse-beat throbbed at the corner of his mouth, his eyes burning into hers.

Slowly his finger ran upwards over the curve of her jaw to settle sensually on her lips. 'And it's not private enough. I couldn't guarantee there'd be no interruptions.' He turned and picked up his briefcase. 'So we go.'

'Where . . . where are we going?' Bree forced her voice out through her constricted throat.

'I have to go out to a site in Ipswich. I can drop you home on the way, or you can come with me for the drive.' His eyes watched her. 'So you do have a choice.'

Bree managed a smile. 'I'd rather come with you,' she said honestly.

His eyebrow rose mockingly and he strode across to open the door, waiting for her to precede him into the outer office.

'Take care of any calls for the rest of the afternoon, Jill,' he instructed his secretary as he crossed with Bree to the elevator.

'Are you familiar with Brisbane?' Heath asked as he headed the Ferrari out along the South-

East Freeway.

'Not, not really. Not this side of the city, anyway. We . . . I lived on a farm on the north side ages ago.'

'When was that?' A faint smile played about his mouth.

'I think I would have been about ten or eleven,' Bree sat happily, liking this easy companionability.

'It was your parents' farm?'

'No,' she replied slowly, choosing her words carefully as she continued. It wouldn't do to give herself away. 'I was a ward of the State and the family who worked the farm fostered me.'

Heath made no comment for a moment as the Ferrari ate up the kilometres.

'Actually, I quite enjoyed being on the farm,' she added tentatively. 'There was a lot of wide open space.'

'You said it was only for a year or two?'

'Yes. I'm not sure what happened really. Maybe the farm wasn't paying its way, but the family had to leave.'

'You didn't go with them?'

'No. I went to another family. In Bundaberg,' she said reflectively.

'How many families fostered you?' he asked quietly.

'I don't remember exactly.' Bree hesitated, not wanting to talk about it in case she slipped up and mentioned Briony.

Heath gave her a sharp look before returning his attention to his driving as they caught up to a group of slower cars.

'Probably about five,' she said at last.

'What happened to your parents?'

'I don't really know. I don't remember my father, but I can vaguely remember my mother. I was five or so when she left ...' Bree caught herself in time before she added 'us'. 'What about you?' she deftly changed the subject. It was so easy to forget she had to guard her tongue when they were sharing this moment of relaxed conversation.

'What about me?' Heath gave a soft lazy laugh that warmed Bree all over.

'Well, you didn't start out as a successful executive, did you?' She spoke lightly.

'Not quite.' Heath was smiling. 'I can't say I remember suffering great hardships. My father died in the first year of my apprenticeship and my mother before I was old enough to remember her.' He pulled out and overtook a slower car. 'A successful executive?' he repeated almost derisively. 'Is that how you see me, Bree?'

'Yes. You are, aren't you? An executive? And I'd say you were very successful, wouldn't you?' she said with a smile.

'Perhaps.' He gave a harsh laugh that shattered the relaxed and easy atmosphere between them. 'But hardly a success in other areas of my life.'

Bree swallowed nervously at the cold cynicism in his tone, not knowing quite what to say, what he expected her to say.

'Maybe we could adapt the old saying to "Lucky in business, unlucky in love".' He glanced sideways at her.

'I don't ... know about that,' Bree stammered.

'I'd say it was pretty applicable. Apart from that, my son and I had such a successful relationship that he drops out and disappears. No, I'm afraid when it comes to Reece I could hardly be called a roaring success.'

'I'm sure that would have been just as much Reece's fault as yours,' Bree ventured.

'Do you? That's very magnanimous of you,' he said a trifle wryly.

'I meant it.' Bree glanced down at her hands as they fingered the seat belt. 'Reece . . . I know Reece could hardly be called deferential, and I guess if it wasn't part of his music or his motorbike he just wasn't interested.'

'But he was interested in you,' Heath said flatly. 'For a time at least.'

Bree turned away to glance out at the passing scenery, a smattering of houses and trees. She had nothing to say to that. There was hardly anything she could say without venturing into deep water. But Heath didn't seem to expect an answer, and they both sat captives of their own thoughts as they reached the more densely settled outskirts of Ipswich.

The construction site was quite near the heart of the commercial section of the coalmining-orientated city, and the project appeared to be well under way, for behind the protective fence the building rose several floors. Heath turned the Ferrari in through the open gates and pulled to a halt in front of a mobile office.

'I'm not sure how long I'll be,' he said, pausing with the car door open before he climbed out from behind the wheel. 'Do you mind waiting?'

Bree shook her head, and after one suddenly firing look that catapulted the emotive scene in Heath's office screamingly back to re-ignite her senses, he swung out of the car and strode across to the office to greet the huge swarthy man wearing a hard safety helmet who met him at the door, and the two men disappeared inside.

Blinking back the blurring tears that flooded her eyes, Bree berated herself for her foolishness. She felt like a puppet on the end of a string, only able to move when the string was pulled. And Heath held the string in his hands.

'Wow! Some wheels!'

The voice brought her out of her self-torturing reverie during which she had alternatively censured and condoned her paltry defences that Heath could storm so effortlessly. She turned sideways to see a young workman wearing a yellow safety helmet eyeing the Ferrari enviously.

'I'd give my eye teeth for one of these beauties!' he grinned, flashing a white smile across his tanned face, and Bree smiled automatically back at him.

'It is pretty smart, isn't it?' she said a little shyly.

'You're not wrong there. Whose is it?' he asked, sinking down on his haunches so that he was on Bree's eye level.

'Heath's. Heath Durant's,' she replied, his name bringing a flush to her cheeks.

'The boss's?' The young man let out a low whistle. 'Didn't know he had one of these. Last time he came up here, he was driving a Mercedes.' The young man's eyes sharpened on Bree. 'You his daughter or something?'

'No. A . . . a friend,' she told him unevenly.

'Oh.' The word had that same knowing ring to it and the young man's eyes flowed over her assessingly, making Bree's lips tighten at his lack of subtlety. 'Nice,' he said ambiguously, a laugh in his voice, his hand running over the smooth paintwork of the car while his eyes still rested on her.

'Porter!' The sound boomed from the direction of the office and the young man started to his feet. 'You want something to do?'

'No, King. Just on my way to get some tools for Reg.' The young man moved off, almost breaking into a trot as Heath's eyes settled heavily on him.

Heath was approaching with the same large swarthy man from the office and he turned to the other man as they reached the car.

'Keep me posted on the situation, King,' he said. 'I'd rather avert more interruptions before things get any worse. We can't let this get out of control. I'll be in touch with Jim Mayor in Toowoomba and have him keep his ear to the ground as well.'

'Okay, Heath.' The big man shook hands with Heath and his dark eyes flicked curiously to Bree, but Heath made no introductions before he strode around and climbed behind the wheel of the Ferrari.

'Are you having some trouble with the building?' Bree asked tentatively as the Ferrari joined the outbound traffic.

'With the building, no,' he replied at last. 'With some of the men, yes.'

'Are they going to strike?'

Heath shrugged. 'They might. However, I'm more worried about the spate of minor accidents that have been occurring lately. King and I suspect someone's out to disrupt the progress of the building, and that unsettles the men.'

'But who would do that?' Bree turned a little sideways in her seat. 'And why?'

'We aim to find out who, and as to the why, it could be anything. Someone bearing a grudge over a lost job is the most likely candidate.' Heath changed gear smoothly. 'What were you and young Porter talking about?' he shot at her out of the blue.

'Porter? That young workman? Nothing really.'
Bree watched his profile and he turned to flash her
a coldly cynical glance. 'He was just admiring your
car, that's all.'

'Just the car? He must have been giving it a
pretty close look-over.' His smile was a faint
shadow of a movement of his lips.

'I assure you, we were talking about the car,'
Bree said evenly.

'You seem to attract them like flies to a
honeypot,' he said with an edge to his voice.

'What do you mean by that?' Bree's own tone
matched his, as his words struck her on the raw.

'Come on, Bree, you know what I'm talking
about. It must have been going on for years.'

'No, I don't know what you're getting at,' Bree
said with ominous quietness. 'Perhaps you'd like
to explain it.'

His eyes flicked over her. 'You have a look that
draws like a magnet, a promise of so much
painted-in innocence. A lot of women would give
the world for lessons in the aura that seems to
come naturally to you.'

'I don't think . . .' she began, but he overrode
her.

'What's the point in denying it? There was
Reece, and that animal at your flat in Sydney,
Glenn back at the car park, and now Porter. God
knows how many others there've been,' he finished
harshly.

Bree could only stare at him speechlessly.

'Well, Bree? Don't we all get drawn into the
web?'

'No!' she burst out. 'I don't . . . How could you
say that?'

'How could I say what?' he repeated mockingly.

'What you're implying.'

He gave a humourless laugh. 'You can ask that after what happened in my office this morning?'

'I didn't . . .' she stopped. She had been going to say that she hadn't wanted him to kiss her, to hold her, to caress her, but that would have been a blatant lie. Even now, if he'd stopped the car, taken her in his arms, she knew she would have weakly and willingly surrendered to him. But he must never know that. 'I wouldn't have . . .'

'Wouldn't have let me make love to you,' he finished as her voice died away. 'Wouldn't you, Bree?' His own voice was a husky arousal.

CHAPTER EIGHT

'No!' The word was a hoarse, restricted sound and Bree swallowed convulsively before she tried again. 'No. I . . . I wouldn't have let you make love to me. I'm not . . .'

'Not that type of girl.' Heath smiled then and slowed the car, pulling into the curb in front of a small shopping centre.

'I don't think that's very funny,' Bree said brokenly, a pain growing in the region of her heart. 'Why are we stopping here? I'd like to go home,' she added with as much calm dignity as she could muster.

'Food,' he said. 'It's past lunch time.'

'I'm not very hungry.' Bree turned away from him, her eyes fixing unseeingly on a stand displaying news headlines.

'Bree.' His voice was soft and he reached out, his fingers taking hold of her chin, turning her head until her eyes met and held his. 'It wasn't funny. I never meant it that way. I'm sorry.'

His incredible blue eyes looked straight into hers and she was powerless to draw her eyes away from the intensity of his. A pulse began to throb in her throat and his thumb moved slowly upwards to touch feather-soft on the curve of her lips. Her breath caught and her mouth came alive beneath his touch. Heath's gaze broke away to run over the fair curtain of her hair, to return to the smoky greyness of her eyes that were held captive by his. The charged air between them began to hum in Bree's ears, the bittersweet tension mounting.

'God—Bree!' His voice was raw and tight, and with a seemingly superhuman effort he dragged his eyes from her and turned away, his hands locked on the steering wheel.

He drew a deep breath. 'Food,' he said with a trace of the same huskiness, and climbed out of his seat to walk around to the passenger side of the car. 'How about a salad roll or something like that?'

Bree nodded unsteadily. 'That will be fine,' she said softly, and after a moment he straightened and strode into a nearby milk-bar-cum-café.

When he returned he handed her a brown paper bag, strapped himself into the car and rejoined the traffic flow. A short time later, as they drove in silence, instead of keeping to the Highway Heath branched off to the left and followed the road through a cluster of houses, past an old two-storied pub, before turning over a narrow bridge that crossed the main Brisbane to Ipswich railway line.

The bitumen road narrowed and snaked through semi-rural pasture to cut between rows of tall old silky oaks and jacaranda trees. Slowing again, Heath turned off the bitumen roadway into a grassy park, stopping the car under a shady tree in a position that afforded them a view of the river some fifty feet below.

'Shall we picnic outside?' He raised one dark eyebrow enquiringly and Bree nodded, smiling as she climbed out of the car to stand gazing at the picturesque panorama of the river and rolling farmland, while Heath shrugged his arms out of his suit coat and thrust it and his tie back into the car. She, too, slipped off her jacket as the warmth of the sun-kissed breeze touched her.

'This is beautiful,' she said as she drew a deep breath. Somewhere someone had been mowing dew-damp grass, and the familiar tang struck a chord from some time in her past. The soft breeze lifted her hair and she smiled easily at Heath as he pulled a checked rug from the boot of the car and laid it on the grass.

Without speaking they sat down on the blanket, using the car's bumper bar as a back-rest, and Bree opened the brown paper bag and pulled out a couple of rolls and two cans of cold soft drink.

Heath looked through the transparent food wrap and grimaced slightly. 'One chicken and one ham and salad each,' he said. 'Hardly up to Lennons, but ideal for a riverside picnic.' He handed her a frosty can of lemonade and began to unwrap his bread roll.

The food was surprisingly good and once she began to eat Bree found she was hungry. She hadn't been able to manage much breakfast, the thought of travelling into the city with Heath churning her stomach, and she made short work of the fresh rolls, washing them down with the cool refreshment of the lemonade.

Replete and more than a little drowsy now, she leant back, listening to the buzz of bees and other insects flying about in the haze of the hot blue sky day. Beside her Heath drained his own can of drink and sighed appreciatively.

'I enjoyed that,' he said as he collected the empty cans and papers and shoved them back into the brown paper bag. As he turned to glance at Bree she stifled a yawn. 'Very peaceful and slumbrous, isn't it?' he smiled, and Bree nodded.

'Beautifully,' she replied. 'And if you kept to the highway you wouldn't even suspect it was here. It's a pity, isn't it?'

'Mmm. This road used to be the main highway out to Ipswich years ago, narrow and not particularly straight as it is.' Heath rested his arm on his drawn-up knee. 'I can remember driving along here with my father in his old Dodge when I was a kid. The trees were all out in flower, the yellow gold of the silky oaks and the mauve of the jacarandas. The fallen blossom from the jacarandas made a carpet of mauve beneath the trees. It was incredible.'

He moved to stretch out his long body, turning a little so that he could use Bree's lap as a pillow. At his touch she tensed, her heart leaping in her chest. She was afraid to meet his eyes, afraid and yet suddenly exhilarated at the expression that those blue eyes might hold. Her gaze skittered downward, but his eyes were closed, his angular features relaxed.

She let herself look at him, her eyes lingering lovingly on each feature. The tousled lock of dark hair falling over his forehead, his dark brows, the fan of thick lashes resting on his cheek, his straight nose, his lips. Her gaze settled on his lips and her own tingled for the touch of his mouth moving so sensuously, so sentiently on hers.

She searched for something in his face that would give her some small sign that would account for the ease with which he could arouse her, why this particular man possessed the power over her no other man ever had. He was attractive, there was no denying that. But so were plenty of other men. Even Reece, who was this man's son, had a sulky sort of good looks, and yet Reece had left

her cold. Her eyes ran over Heath's features again,
now seeking some small resemblance between
father and son, but she could find none.

With a will of their own her eyes slipped
downwards to the faint rhythmic rise and fall of
his chest, his shirt partially undone to display the
light covering of dark body hair. How she longed
to have the freedom to feel her fingertips moving
through the curling dark hair peppered here and
there with grey, to slide her hand across the
flatness of his stomach. Her gaze dropped lower,
down to the muscular thighs moulded by his
tailored slacks and she grew hot at her lustful
thoughts.

But were they purely wanton? This wanting to
have Heath make love to her felt as natural to her
as the need to breathe. Deep inside her she
throbbed to have the long sleek length of him
moving with her. And no man had made her feel
like that.

As the depth of her feelings rose to send her
heart thumping in her breast her eyes went back to
his face, a tide of yearning washing over her. She
wouldn't have believed she could fall in love so
quickly, so irrevocably. Before she could stay its
movement her hand went to smooth back the lock
of thick hair from his forehead and he stirred
slightly, making an appreciative murmur deep in
his chest, the corners of his mouth lifting in a lazy
smile. Mortified, Bree snatched her hand away,
but Heath's eyes opened a fraction so that he
could capture her hand in his, carrying it slowly to
his lips. He placed a soft kiss in her palm and then
transferred her hand to his chest, his own fingers
keeping it there.

If the world had chosen that precise moment to

stop turning Bree knew she would have scarcely
noticed the conjecturable fall from it, for nothing
she could imagine could match the soaring of her
senses at Heath's tender caress.

Her fingers curled against the silkiness of his
shirt and her fingertips stole beneath its partially
unbuttoned front to touch his skin. His eyes
opened to look up at her, and embarrassed at her
daring, she slid her hand back so that the thin
material separated her seeking fingers from his
body. Unable to meet his gaze, she swallowed
nervously, knowing his eyes hadn't left her face.
The air between them crackled with the same
aroused awareness.

Heath's fingers moved to undo the remaining
buttons on his shirt and he shifted her hand until it
was splayed out over his tanned midriff.

'Touch me, Bree!' His throaty tone was as
deeply sensual as his words, and she needed no
second bidding to allow herself to luxuriate in the
heady sensation of the texture of his firm skin
beneath her fingers.

His own hand moved to slide slowly up the
length of her bare arm, over her shoulder, to twist
in the spill of her hair. He groaned softly as her
fingers audaciously skimmed the waistband of his
pants and his hand behind her head bent her down
until his lips found hers, captured them, and she
opened her mouth against his as their mutual
passion flared, flamed to engulf them.

With a minimum of pressure Heath brought her
down to stretch out beside him, his fingers
caressing her sensitive earlobe, the curve of her
throat, to steal with slow erogenousness downwards until his hand cupped her breast, found her
tautening nipple through the material of her top.

All at once that material was a superfluous barrier and he lifted the waistband so that his hands moved over her bare skin. Shifting her slightly, he unhooked the catches on her bra, freeing her breasts to the touch of his fingers.

Bree moaned, her hands sliding across his shoulders beneath his loosened shirt, her own fingers curling into his firm flesh. Her body strained against him, the swell of his hard arousal arching her impossibly closer.

Heath's lips flowed over the bared rise of her breast to reach a taut peak and she ran her tongue tip upwards along the curve of his throat, her teeth nibbling his earlobe. She was beyond conscious thought. She had gone beyond anything, existing only in the sensual nuances of Heath's body, the shattering wonder of his caresses.

Shakily her fingers found the buckle of his belt, pulling it loose, her fingers burning downwards, and his arms tightened about her, his lips lost in the valley between her breasts. And then he had released her, his hand staying hers at his waist. His eyes consumed hers and she could see the reflection of her own blazing arousal in their inky blue depths.

'Bree! We'd better cool down,' he muttered huskily, 'unless you want us to get arrested.' His mouth held a shadow of a mocking smile, although his face was still flushed, tension in the hard line of his jaw.

His words restored part of her sensibility and she felt the hot colour flood her cheeks as she recalled the open publicity of the park. Anyone could have seen them. Her hand went unsteadily to pull down her shirt to cover her nakedness. Heath's lips tightened, his hand halting her, his

head lowering to take first one still aroused nipple
in his mouth and then the other.

'God, Bree, I want you!' he said thickly. 'I want
to make love to you more than I've wanted any
woman. I want to caress you, kiss every inch of
your beautiful body.' He pulled her shirt down to
cover her breasts and sat up. 'Come on, let's go.'

Holding out his hand, he pulled her into a
sitting position and then they were both standing,
his arms encircling her, holding her against him so
that she could feel the ardour burning in him just
as strongly.

'Go where?' she mouthed bemusedly through
swollen lips.

'To a motel. There's one on the highway near
here,' he replied, his fingers teasing the sensitive
nerve-endings along her spine.

'A motel,' Bree breathed, the words acting like a
douche of cold water. 'A motel? No!' She began to
shake her head. 'No!' Her voice broke.

His body was still and tense, his hands on her
not moving now as his eyes ranged down on her.

'I don't want to go ... to go to a motel,' she
choked, filled with a disgust that was directed as
much at herself as it was at him, making her feel
cheap and sordid.

'Why not?' Heath's voice was cold and even.

'Because ...' Bree shook her head again, her
hair falling forward to shield her face and the
blurring rush of tears to her eyes. 'How could you
ask me to?' Her voice caught on a sob.

His fingers tightened painfully momentarily
before he thrust her away from him to run a hand
through his hair. 'It's a hell of a lot more private
than this park,' he ground out.

'Don't say that!' Bree cringed at the recalled

realisation that she had been so lost in her own sensuality that she had been totally unaware of her surroundings.

'Why not? And what's so wrong with a motel?' His face was pale with anger. 'You were more than willing to make love right here a few moments ago. Or is that it, Bree? Do you like the added excitement it entails?' His hands grabbed her again, hauling her against him. 'Well, is that it? Are you something of an exhibitionist, my love?' he sneered.

'No!' she cried. 'Please, Heath, stop it. You're hurting me!' His fingers were bruising her waist and she pushed ineffectually against his chest.

'Hurting you?' He swore angrily. 'Well, if you prefer this to a motel then who am I to knock it?' he added, his lips crushing hers in a savage assault.

Bree whimpered in her throat as he bent her backwards over the low bonnet of the car. She fought against him, her hands beating on his back until her strength left her and she lay quiescent beneath the pressure of his body, tears pouring down to dampen her hair, her chest heaving agonisedly beneath him with her sobs.

His punishment ceased as suddenly as it had started and he stood back, pulling her upright, his hands dropping from her, and she stood swaying before him. Turning away from her, his body heaving as he drew deep steadying breaths, he began to tuck his shirt back into his trousers. Bree stood numbly, waiting until he slowly turned back to her and she could see he now had himself under tight control. It was in the lines of his body, the cold remoteness of his rugged face.

'I suppose I should apologise for that,' he said, his lips thinning as she hurriedly dashed the dampness of tears from her cheeks. 'Put it down to unleashed frustration,' he grimaced.

'I'm sorry, too,' she murmured. 'I shouldn't have . . . I never meant to . . .' she floundered for words.

Heath bent down to gather up the rug. 'Let's not hold a post-mortem. I think we'd better be getting home, don't you?' he said flatly, not looking at her, and Bree almost fell into the car, fumbling to straighten her clothing before he joined her.

The journey home was completed in silence, a heavy, wearing nerve-racking silence, that had Bree's stomach churning nauseously. She didn't dare to look at him, feeling his anger. And he had every right to be angry with her, she accused herself, sick with self-revulsion.

Heath drove with a cold restraint and when at last they pulled up in front of the house he left the engine running, leaning across her to flick open her door. His arm didn't touch her as she shrank back, but she felt her traitorous body's response to his nearness and she all but threw herself out of the car.

'Mmm, nothing like a nice cup of tea,' said Peg as she drained her cup, keeping a motherly eye on Ben as he played happily on his rug in the shade beside her. She had brought a tray out into the garden, and Bill had finished his tea and returned to his pruning while Bree sat in the sun drying her hair in readiness for the party that evening.

'Have you decided how you're going to wear your hair tonight?' Peg asked as Bree ran her brush through the nearly dry cloud of her fair hair that shone in the sunlight.

'I usually just wear it loose. It's a little hard to keep it up when it's just been washed,' she replied, her heart catching its beat at the thought of being alone again with Heath. They had barely spoken since he dropped her home the previous day and she only had to think about recalling that scene by the river for her to blush profusely.

'I'm glad Heath's taking you to the party,' Peg was saying. 'You should get out more often, and you know Ben's safe with me,' she added as Bree glanced at the baby.

'I do know that, Peg, and I'm grateful for your offer but, well, I don't . . .' She sighed. 'To tell you the truth, Peg, I'm not looking forward to tonight. I haven't been to a party for months, in fact, I somehow don't think I'll ever have been to Heath's kind of party, and I guess I'm a little nervous about it. I mean, I won't know anyone and I'll feel strange with Heath's friends.'

'Now, now! There's no need to get all worked up about that. Heath will look after you, and as far as his friends go—well, most of those I've met have been really nice folk. You'll enjoy it, you'll see,' Peg assured her.

'I hope so.' Bree was doubtful. She'd never mixed with the type of people she imagined would be Heath's contemporaries and she rather suspected she was going to feel like the proverbial country bumpkin. For sure, they would all be sophisticated, and even in the clothes that had been delivered from the boutique Bree knew she was going to feel like a fish out of water.

How she wished she possessed the poise and self-assurance of Roslyn Jacobs! She had a picture of the owner of the boutique and Heath together, and a pain jabbed at her sensitive heart. They would make such a striking couple, and the other woman would never have allowed the mere thought of a prospective party to have her quivering inside like a jelly. Roslyn was more Heath's style, more in keeping with his successful image. While she, Bree, could never hope to match a man like Heath Durant.

She sighed dejectedly. If Heath married again it would be to someone of the Roslyn Jacobs type, not a naïve inexperienced nobody like Bree Ransome. And then she wondered about his wife, Reece's mother. Had she been like Roslyn? Pamela and Heath had to have been married when they were both quite young, so maybe they had grown up together, first young love.

'Peg, what was Heath's wife like?' She turned to the older woman without thinking, and then it was too late to take back the question.

'Pamela?' Peg's lips thinned.

'You knew her, didn't you?'

'Oh, yes. I knew Pamela,' she replied bitterly, and Bree's eyebrows rose in surprise at her tone. 'And I'd rather not have met her.'

CHAPTER NINE

'I'M sorry.' Bree felt dreadful. 'I . . . I didn't mean to pry—I just wondered what she was like.'

'I don't mind you asking, love,' Peg reassured her. 'it's only that I can't even think about that woman without getting angry. The dance she led poor Heath! I know it's not nice to speak ill of the dead, but that woman was . . .' Peg shook her head. 'She was the most selfish, self-centred person I've ever met.'

'She was . . . Mr Hailey said she was very beautiful,' Bree said softly.

Peg's frown deepened. 'Beauty is as beauty does. She was never a wife to Heath, and she was only a mother to Reece when she thought it would get at his father. It's no wonder the boy . . .' she stopped. 'Well, no matter, I suppose I shouldn't gossip, but I can't pretend there was ever any love lost between Pamela and myself. If it hadn't been for Heath Bill and I would never have stayed on.'

'Heath said she died seven years ago. What happened to her?'

Peg's eyes fell away and she picked up a soft toy to attract Ben's attention. 'She died in a car accident not far from here.'

Bree was silent, piecing all that Peg had said and hadn't said together. If Peg was to be believed then Heath's marriage had been far from happy. Was it any wonder he had never remarried? And if his parents had been unhappy perhaps part of Reece's

145

attitude to life was some reflection of his disturbed
family life.

But at some stage Heath must have been in love
with Pamela, or else he would never have married
her in the first place. Unless ... What was it
Ranald Hailey had implied? That Heath had only
married Pamela to gain some standing in his
father-in-law's firm. Was Heath capable of doing
that?

His strong face swam in her mind's eye, all hard
craggy angles, ruggedly attractive, but cold and
uncompromising, too. To become the success he
was, to have built his construction business up to
the multi-million-dollar operation it obviously was
today, then Heath Durant must have a certain
amount of steel in his character to go with the
solid business astuteness. Perhaps in his climb of
personal ambition marrying the boss's daughter
was an acceptable price to pay. No, Heath would
never ...

Bree stared at herself in the huge mirror on
her dressing table mulling it all over once again.
How could she really say what type of man
Heath was? All she knew of him was the touch
of his hands, his lips caressing hers, the movement of his body against hers. A slow flush crept
into her pale cheeks, adding colour to her light
make-up.

She had been ready for the party for a good
quarter of an hour, but she was loath to leave the
sanctuary of her room. Her mirror reflected the
fact that she had never looked better. But then
again, as she reminded herself mockingly, she had
never before had at her disposal the type of clothes
she was wearing now. This dress and matching
high-heeled sandals probably equalled in cost the

entire wardrobe she had packed in the battered suitcase in the flat in Sydney.

Her eyes moved downwards again and she couldn't quell the quiver of excitement she felt, knowing that the dress suited her so well. It was black and the soft material was clinging enough to more than hint at the firm fullness of her breasts, the narrowness of her waist, the rounded curve of her hips, and the length flattered the long shapeliness of her legs. The halter-style bodice showed her lightly tanned shoulders to perfection and the neckline plunged to shadow the valley between her breasts.

Her hair shone like shot silk, falling down her back in a glittering cascade, the one wave in its straightness curving away from her forehead at her off-centre parting. The little eye-shadow and mascara she had applied emphasised the luminous smoky greyness of her eyes and the gloss on her trembling lips was an unconscious temptation.

She heard Heath's footsteps leave his room and pass along the hall to the living-room and knew she would have to join him. Touching on a little perfume, she smiled wryly at the bottle. It was a relatively inexpensive brand available from any chain store, but she liked its subtle muskiness and it gave her a small spurt of courage. Somehow it was her link with yesterday, with the Bree Ransome she had been before she met Heath Durant.

'Are you ready, love?' Peg tapped on her door. 'Heath's waiting.'

'Yes. I'm coming now.' With one last look at her reflection Bree squared her shoulders and crossed to the door.

'My, don't you look stunning!' Peg beamed at

her as they walked along the short hallway and entered the living-room. 'Doesn't Bree look beautiful, Heath?'

His eyes made a quick assessment, bringing colour flooding to Bree's cheeks, and the corners of his mouth flicked upwards. 'Absolutely,' he said evenly, and took a gulp of the drink in the glass he held, the expression in his eyes now shielded by his lashes. 'Shall we go?' He set the empty glass on the coffee table.

'You might need a jacket for coming home,' remarked Peg. 'It can be cool later on in the evening.'

'Do you think I will, Peg?' Bree began.

'I'll make sure she doesn't catch cold,' Heath smiled at the older woman. 'We'll see you in the morning. Don't wait up for us.'

'Where is the party being held?' Bree asked at last.

They had been driving for some time in what was for her an uneasy silence, one that filled the car with far too vivid memories of their drive, and its passion-filled aftermath, of the day before.

'Toowong,' he answered. 'The end of this street, in fact.'

'Who's ᵧ. who will be there?' Her voice broke with her nervousness.

'Probably an assortment coming and going,' he said lightly.

'Oh.'

'What's the matter?' he asked as he swung the Ferrari around and backed neatly into the kerb in front of a two-storeyed house, the bottom storey concealed behind a high white brick fence. Branches of large spreading poinciana trees overhung the fence and a white wrought-iron gate gave entrance through an archway on to the property.

'I'm just a little nervous of meeting your friends, that's all,' she told him honestly.

He gave a soft harsh cynical laugh. 'Acquaintances. Very few I'd count as friends.'

Bree watched him as he lit a cigarette. 'But I thought the party was being given by a friend of yours.'

'It's just a party.' He drew on his cigarette and the end glowed red in the dimness of the car's interior. 'A highly social affair if it runs true to form,' he added, 'and always in aid of a good charitable cause.'

'You don't sound very enthusiastic about going,' she remarked, and he shrugged and glanced across at her.

'There are other things I'd prefer to spend my time doing,' he said huskily, and she felt his eyes touching her, starting that same fire. 'But that could lead over dangerous ground,' he added softly.

Bree's heart began beating an irregular tattoo at the sensual innuendo in his lowered tone. 'Who's giving the party?' she asked to cover the confusion that had gripped her.

Heath drew on his cigarette and then stubbed it out in the ashtray before answering. 'Roslyn Jacobs,' he said flatly as he climbed out of the car.

Bree waited for him to open her own door and then stood on the footpath as he bent to lock the car. Her hands nervously smoothed the folds of her dress as she faced the evening with even less enthusiasm, not looking forward at all to renewing her acquaintance with Roslyn Jacobs.

Heath took her arm, starting her towards the

ornate arched gate, his hand sliding around until it
rested on her bare arm as she moved. At the shaft
of light slanting through the gateway her steps
faltered and Heath's fingers tightened, taking them
inside the walled garden.

'Heath, I . . .' Bree held back as they approached
the wide front steps.

Stopping, Heath turned to gaze down at her, his
eyes falling over the agitated rise and fall of her
breasts.

'I'm not sure I want to go,' she got out.

'And I'm not sure I want you to either,' he said
wryly. 'That dress is,' he paused, 'very becoming.'
His hand moved gently over her waist, his eyes
burning down to rest on her lips, and she caught
her breath at her body's response.

'Heath darling! You're here!' A feminine voice
hailed him from the open doorway, breaking the
highly-charged bond that held them immobile, and
as Roslyn Jacobs appeared on the small patio
Heath moved Bree forward to climb the few steps.

Tall and slender in a dark catsuit, Roslyn gave
Bree one all-consuming look before she turned her
attention back to Heath.

'I'm so glad you made it,' she purred, holding
her hands out to him, and Heath took them,
smiling.

'You remember Bree, Roslyn.' He disengaged
himself and drew Bree forward.

Roslyn smiled faintly. 'Of course. The dress is
superb, dear.' She turned back to Heath. 'Come
on inside and join everyone.'

They moved inside and Bree had time to notice
that the house was an interior decorator's dream
before she was propelled into what seemed like a
whirling crowd of people. Some talked, gesticulat-

ing with the drinks in their hands, while others danced to the pulsating music. Everywhere there was movement, and Bree wished she could take hold of Heath's arm and not let him go. But he managed to keep her beside him, for which she was profoundly thankful, although the openly curious stares they were given had her cringing with embarrassment.

A couple of people hailed him and he introduced her, but she felt out of place and any conversation she might have made dried up inside her. She shouldn't have come. She could never be part of this crowd of colourful people.

And then she was separated from Heath as a laughing group surged past them, and her eyes searched panic-stricken for his dark head. Her stomach churned and she knew she'd paled as her eyes flicked desperately about her. The noise seemed to crowd in on her and for an awful minute she thought she was going to faint away.

'I'm here.' His deep voice reduced her legs to water and as she turned thankfully to find him beside her, her hand reached out instinctively to clutch his arm in her relief.

'Oh, Heath!' Her voice came out low and uneven as she gazed up at him with trembling lips.

His fingers covered hers where they rested on his arm and his thumb rubbed slowly over the back of her hand. 'Bree!' Her name was a physical caress that isolated them from the crowds filling the room and the noise seemed to fade off into the distance. 'If you look at me like that,' his fingers tightened on hers, 'we'll have to go somewhere and find a party of our own, just the two of us!'

His gaze held a burning glow she recognised, that set her senses spinning with facile intimacy, that had her wanting him as much as his deep blue eyes were telling her that he wanted her. 'In fact, that wouldn't be a bad idea.'

'Well, here you are, you two!' Ranald Hailey's voice crashed over them as he slapped Heath on the back. 'I was beginning to think you hadn't turned up.' His pale eyes went from Heath's taut features to the wash of colour that rose in Bree's cheeks. 'You look divine, my dear.' He carried her hand to his lips with a flourish. 'Doesn't she, old man?'

Heath's head moved slightly in mocking agreement.

'I've brought someone over to meet you,' Ranald drew a younger man forward. 'Someone more your own age. We don't want you bored to death talking to us old fogies all night.'

Bree couldn't summon up the nerve to see how Heath had taken Ranald's comment and she made herself smile as a tall, good-looking young man stepped forward.

'This is Alan Paine. He's George Paine's son,' Ranald added for Heath's benefit. 'He's just back from the States. Alan, meet Bree Ransome and Heath Durant.'

'Hi!' Alan Paine had a nice cleancut face and his eyes moved over Bree with admiration. He held out his hand to Heath. 'How do you do, sir. I believe you know my father?'

'Yes, I do. Quite well, as a matter of fact.' Heath shook hands with the young man and Bree stole a sideways glance at him. All trace of the arousal that had reached out from him to hold her just minutes ago had gone as he nodded aloofly at Alan Paine.

'We'll leave these young people to get acquainted, shall we?' suggested Ranald Hailey.

'Besides, Heath, I see George over there. He wants to talk to you about your trip south. Seems he's having trouble with those same suppliers.'

With one level inscrutable glance from Bree to the young man at her side Heath moved off with the other man.

Alan Paine was quick to take advantage of having Bree's sole attention, and he soon put her at her ease so that she relaxed completely and began to draw him out about his trip to the United States. He was quite amusing, making her laugh at his keen descriptions of different hilarious happenings on his holiday.

When he suggested they dance she readily agreed. Most of the music was modern, and Alan danced easily without selfconsciousness, his eyes smilingly admiring Bree. After a while the music slowed to a quieter number and Alan pulled her lightly into his arms. She enjoyed moving with him and he made no attempt to use the intimacy of the dance the way some young men she had met in the past would have done.

Relaxed, Bree smiled up at him and then through a break in the crowd her eyes locked with a pair of steely blue ones. Even across the room she could feel the unleashed anger burning in their depths.

She shivered slightly and Alan glanced down at her, his eyebrows rising enquiringly.

'What's the matter? Not cold, are you?' he asked.

'No—it's nothing. Somebody walked over my grave.' She forced a laugh. 'I guess I'm just a little tired. Do you mind if we sit down?'

'Of course not.' He led her out of the dancers. 'How about a drink?'

'That would be nice. Perhaps an orange juice?'
Bree sank into a large lounge chair that was
miraculously vacant and Alan left her to get the
drinks.

'Are you enjoying yourself?' Heath's voice came
from behind her and, momentarily startled, she
twisted her head up to look at him.

'Yes, I am.' Her voice dried up on her.

Heath took a mouthful of the drink he held and
grimaced into the amber liquid. 'You appear to
have discovered a——' he paused, 'friend,' he
finished mockingly, and Bree could only look up
at him, her stomach twisting at his jibe. 'The two
of you seemed to find plenty to talk about.'

'He was telling me about his trip. He's,' Bree
swallowed, 'he's been in the United States for three
months.'

'So his father tells me.' His eyes were mere slits
as they bore broodingly down on her. 'He's a nice-
looking boy, don't you think?'

'I guess he is.' Bree agreed softly, and it
occurred to her that perhaps Heath was jealous.
Her heartbeats thudded, echoing inside her. What
would he say if she told him honestly that as far as
she was concerned no one came close to holding a
candle to him?

'Has he asked you out?' He swirled the drink
around his glass.

Bree frowned. 'No, of course not! We haven't
. . . I scarcely know him.'

His eyes held hers and she shifted in her seat
to ease the crick in her neck from looking up at
him.

'You scarcely knew me either,' he said, his voice
low, his lips twisting cynically.

'That's different . . .' she began.

'Different?' He raised one mocking dark brow. 'How, different?'

'It just is.' Bree swallowed. How could she explain that she felt she'd known Heath for ever?

Whatever he would have said to that she wasn't to know, for at that moment Alan returned to hand her a glass of orange juice. He had a Coke for himself, and as Bree thanked him he smiled at her.

'Well, I have an early appointment in the morning.' Heath glanced irritatedly at his wristwatch. 'I think I'll call it a night.'

Bree struggled from the sunken depths of the chair and Alan leaned forward to help her, his hand on her arm, showing surprise when Bree made it obvious she would be leaving with Heath.

'Do you have to go, too?' he asked her, and she nodded.

'Pity,' he shrugged goodnaturedly. 'Well, I guess it's goodnight. I've really enjoyed talking to you, Bree.'

'What! Leaving already?' Ranald Hailey materialised beside Alan.

'Mr Durant has an early appointment,' Alan told him.

'There's no need for you to leave too, is there, Bree? Not when you're having such a good time. I'm sure Alan would be pleased to drop you home.' Ranald put a hand on Alan's shoulder and Bree wondered if she imagined the sly smile he snaked at Heath.

'Oh, no. Thank you.' Bree glanced at Heath, but she could gauge none of his thoughts from his expressionless face. 'I'm feeling a little tired. I think I'll go now with Heath.'

'Okay. Perhaps you'd care to have dinner with

me one evening?' Alan suggested, slanting a sideways look in Heath's direction. 'Maybe tomorrow night, if you're free?'

'I . . .' Bree began to refuse.

'Bree's already booked for tomorrow night,' Heath cut in. 'She's dining with me.'

'Oh. Oh, well, maybe some other time.' Alan shifted uneasily as Heath's eyes rested coldly on him.

'Thank you for the invitation, anyway.' Bree gave him a small smile, trying to take the tension from the atmosphere which had become brittle at Heath's chilling statement.

'Ready?' Heath took Bree's arm. 'We'll see you around.' He nodded to Ranald Hailey and Alan as he moved Bree towards the door. Roslyn Jacobs caught his eyes and he raised a hand in farewell, not acknowledging the fact that she obviously wanted to speak to him.

Outside, he unlocked the car in silence and they had turned on to the main arterial road before he spoke.

'Do I have to apologise?' he asked drily.

'You were a little rude to Alan,' Bree began.

'I felt rude.' He accelerated through an intersection on a green light.

'Alan didn't mean anything by asking me out. He was only being friendly,' she told him defensively.

Heath gave a soft laugh but made no comment and they drove on in an uncomfortable silence. At that hour, well after midnight, the road was relatively free of traffic and they arrived home in no time.

Once inside Heath flicked on the softly glowing wall bracket lights in the living-room. Crossing to the small bar, he poured himself a drink while Bree stood watching him uncertainly. He glanced across at her and downed the drink in one mouthful, turning to pour another.

'Heath.' She spoke his name softly and took a tentative step towards him. 'Heath, don't you think it's a little late for . . . for that?'

He gave a harsh humourless laugh. 'A little late for what exactly?' he asked suggestively, his eyes running insolently over her, and she flushed.

'You said you had an early appointment.'

'It seemed a good excuse at the time.' He raised the glass to his lips.

She watched him warily for a moment, sensing a controlled inexplicable fury about him, volatile for all that.

'I'm . . . I'm tired. I think I'll go to bed,' she said at last.

'What a good idea.' His eyes settled on her lips. 'I was about to suggest it myself.' His voice was almost frozen. Setting his half empty glass on the bar-top, he strode measuredly across to her.

Bree stepped instinctively backwards, her breath catching in alarm. 'Please, Heath. No!' Her hand went up to fend him off, but he hauled her roughly to him, moving his hard body insinuatingly against her.

'No? Don't you mean yes?' His eyes burned down on her trembling lips. 'Maybe then I might find some peace,' he added softly, his voice deeply ragged, and his lips crushed hers.

The pain of his savage assault brought a rush of tears to her eyes and when he eventually raised his head her sobs caught tearingly in her throat. Heath was breathless and his eyes raked her wet face. Swearing, he thrust her away from him, turning his back on her, one hand rubbing the tension in his neck.

'Go to bed, Bree,' he said flatly, all the anger absent now from his voice.

'Heath?' she said his name in a whisper, and he looked back over his shoulder at her. And his face was pale in the subdued lighting.

'I said go to bed.' He crossed to the bar. 'Just get out of my sight before I do something we'll both regret.'

CHAPTER TEN

THROUGHOUT the next morning Bree's stomach churned nervously. She had purposely remained in her room until she heard Heath drive away so that she didn't have to face him. Cowardly, she knew, but she needed time to get herself together after the emotion-sapping scene of last night.

She had seen Heath angry before, but not as portentously restrained, as close to losing his control as he had been when they returned from the party, and she shivered as she sat in the warm sunshine watching Ben's attempts to stand up by himself.

How ever was she going to face an evening alone with Heath? The more time she spent with him the weaker she became as far as resisting him was concerned. Her biggest battle was with herself. A little voice urged her to take what she could while she could, but she knew that was impossible to do and still retain what little self-respect she had left.

Besides, once he discovered she wasn't the baby's mother, that she had deceived him, no matter how good her intentions had been, then he would cast her aside. If she told him the truth now, explained before he found out . . .

Bree rubbed her hand over her eyes and sighed dejectedly. Maybe Heath would forget about his invitation to dinner. When it all boiled down to it he hadn't actually asked her to go.

The phone rang inside the house and a few minutes later Peg came out on to the patio.

'That was Heath, love,' she frowned. 'Wouldn't you know he's had to rush off to Toowoomba and doesn't think he'll make it back tonight. He said to tell you he's sorry, but he'll have to postpone your dinner engagement this evening.'

'Oh!' A mixture of relief and regret flowed over her and she insisted to herself that it was most definitely mainly relief.

'Disappointing, isn't it?' commiserated Peg. 'But Heath will make it up to you, you'll see.' She frowned again. 'I think he's having a worrying time with his business at the moment. He seems so tense and tired these days.' She shook her head and went to walk back inside as the phone rang again. She returned straight away to inform Bree the call was for her.

'Who is it?' Bree asked in surprise as she scooped Ben up and handed him to Peg.

'I don't know. A young man.' Peg was obviously trying not to show her disapproval, and Bree hurried inside.

'Hi, Bree! It's Alan—Alan Paine.'

Bree forced her hand to relax on the receiver. 'Oh, hello, Alan,' She shifted nervously, conscious of Peg hovering in the background.

'How are you? Over the party?'

'Yes. I'm fine.'

'Good,' he said, sounding pleased with himself. 'I'm just looking to capitalise on Mr Durant's misfortune,' he laughed. 'Seeing as he had to rush up to Toowoomba they let me take over his booking at the restaurant, so I'm offering to take you instead, since he'll be tied up. How about it?'

'I don't know, Alan. I really don't feel up to it tonight,' she began, wondering how Alan came to know Heath had had to leave town. Unless Heath had told him. A pain squeezed at her heart at the implications behind that thought.

'Course you will,' Alan was saying. 'I guess I won't be as distinguished company as Mr Durant would have been, but I promise to give it a try.'

'Well . . .' Bree hesitated. Was there an underlying insinuation in Alan's words, as though he was intimating that there was something between Heath and herself? Bree swallowed. 'I . . . I wouldn't want to be late, Alan.'

'Fine by me. I'm still a bit jet-lag prone. But I'm really looking forward to tonight, Bree. Thanks for coming. I'll see you at seven.' He hung up.

Bree slowly replaced the receiver, wondering if she had been manoeuvred into accepting Alan's invitation or if she was seeing bogey-men who weren't there.

The Fountain Room in Brisbane's Cultural Centre was the most quietly opulent restaurant Bree had ever seen, had ever imagined, from its off-white walls to the thick pale salmon carpet on the split-level floor. The seats were of a matching salmon upholstery and set around small white-clothed tables. Each of the three levels had its own intimate cluster of tables, and planters of tropical green ferns and palms added colour to the decor.

They were escorted to a table for two by the wall of glass panels that displayed a view of the Brisbane River and the city centre. Coloured lighting from the multi-storeyed buildings threw variegated patterns on the water, and as they were seated a gaily lit cruise boat motored up river. White lights lit the freeway lining the river bank and the spanning arches of the Victoria Bridge off to the right, and the Jubilee Fountain glowed gushes of gold between the restaurant and the bridge.

Bree gazed about her, feeling glad she had chosen the outfit she wore. Her mulberry tailored slacks, and matching knitted sleeveless top and complementary-toned floral chiffon over-blouse that was caught by one button at the waist, was not out of place in the elegantly dressed groups of diners already seated.

'Pretty impressive, isn't it?' asked Alan as the immaculately dressed waiter placed Bree's serviette across her lap.

'I didn't realise Brisbane was so picturesque.' Bree could scarcely take her eyes from the view.

'Well, night time and bright lights can hide the rough edges,' laughed Alan,' but it's the only place I can call home.'

'Have you lived here all your life?' Bree asked as the waiter set a colourfully arranged bowl of fresh salad, crisp lettuce, celery curls, cucumber and carrot spears on the table and handed them their menus with a flourish that was in keeping with the whole tone of the restaurant.

'All my life,' Alan nodded. 'Although I have travelled about a bit—Europe, Asia and the U.S. I guess now I have to do a stretch of settling down. Dad's been pretty good letting me sow my wild oats, but now I'll have to start learning the trade, so to speak. We've got a construction company much like Mr Durant's. Not quite as big, though.'

He chatted on about himself and his family. He was twenty-four, he told her, and had two younger sisters. Bree was happy to sit and listen to his conversation. He had an unmalicious sense of humour which was more often than not self-directed, and by the time the main course was served she realised she was enjoying herself and was pleased she had allowed him to talk her into coming out. At home she would only have sat and brooded.

The grilled fish Bree had chosen was delicious, and it was some time before she noticed that the waiter kept topping up her glass and that the unaccustomed wine had begun to loosen her tongue.

'So you hail from Bundaberg, up in the sugar country.' Alan remarked, obviously enjoying his own serve of seasoned steak. 'What did you do up there?'

'I worked in a small art and craft supplies shop when I left school, and then I——' Bree paused, 'I went down to Sydney for a while but couldn't find a job there, so I went back to Bundaberg.'

'Is that where you met Mr Durant?' he asked casually enough, though he flicked her a sharp glance.

'No.' Bree searched about for some way of changing the subject and took a shaky sip of her wine. Should she mention Reece, or would that only lead to more complications? Ah, what a tangled web, she thought wryly.

'My father admires the way Mr Durant runs his business. Every project he touches seems to turn to gold. Mr Durant built his company up from practically nothing, you know, so you can't help but admire him. I suppose you'd call him a self-made man.' Alan shook his head. 'And wow! That red Ferrari of his!' He touched his fingers to his lips expressively. 'Superb! What's it like to drive in it?'

'As you said,' Bree smiled, 'superb.'

'What I wouldn't give for one of those—but I'm

stuck with my old M.G., at least until I've made a
bit of cash. Ran Hailey said Mr Durant has a
Mercedes as well?'

'Yes, he has. But Bill Roland usually drives
that.'

'If I said "idle rich" it would only be pure envy,'
Alan laughed. 'I mean, he may be rich, but you
couldn't call Mr Durant idle.'

'No. He works long hours,' Bree agreed.

'My father's like that, too. Works like two men.
But I guess they both enjoy it.' Alan shrugged.
'Now take Ran Hailey, he's what's known as one
of the idle rich. I sometimes wonder when he does
actually work.'

'What does he do?' Bree asked. Although she
had no interest in Ranald Hailey she was pleased
to be off the subject of Heath Durant.

'Some sort of accountant, I think. His father
and his uncle built up the firm and he inherited it.'
Alan paused while the waiter removed their plates.
'They've all known each other for years,' he
remarked as the waiter left them, and Bree raised
her eyebrows enquiringly. 'My father, Ran Hailey
and Mr Durant,' he explained. 'My father and
Ran went to school together, with Mr Durant's
wife.'

'Oh.' Bree glanced down at her wine glass.

The waiter was a welcome interruption as he
returned carrying a tray of the most delicious-
looking desserts she had ever seen. Alan chose a
huge slice of apple pie topped with cream, but Bree
had to shake her head.

'They look divine,' she smiled up at the young
waiter, 'but I just couldn't fit it in. Perhaps some
tea?' she asked shyly.

'Of course.' The waiter moved away and came

back with a silver tea service and a plate of petits fours, miniature chocolate éclairs, coconut macaroons and cream puffs.

Bree's exclamation of delight turned the conversation to other restaurants Alan had dined at, and he didn't mention Heath Durant again. They lingered over their tea and coffee, and Alan took her arm when they eventually made a move to leave. His hand found hers as they strolled slowly back to Alan's car.

'What would you like to do now?' he asked as he slid into the driver's seat beside her. 'Hey—I know! If you're not familiar with Brisbane at night how about we drive up to the best touristy lookout for a view of the city?'

'Well, if it's not too far I suppose we could,' Bree said, really longing to be taken home. But after the delicious meal she hadn't the heart to cut Alan's evening short.

'It's on the way home anyway,' Alan grinned as he started the car, the inadequate suppressor causing the engine noise to echo around the closed-in car park. 'We go out past the new Botanic Gardens and Planetarium,' he raised his voice. 'Been out there?'

Bree shook her head.

'Right. Straight up Mount Coot-tha.' He backed the car out of the park.

The wind tugged at the scarf Bree had tied around her hair and she was glad of the jacket Peg had lent her as Alan headed the open sports car out of the city. He pointed out the large floodlit tropical display dome made of aluminium and glass set amid the Botanic Gardens and the almost futuristic curves of the Planetarium. Then the road wound up the mountain and Bree clutched the edges of her seat as Alan swung the car around the hairpin bends.

He parked at the top and climbed out over the closed door. 'Come on over to the observation look-out.' He took her hand.

And he was right about the view. The lights of the city and suburbs were spread out below them as far as they could see. Alan put his arm around her shoulders as he pointed out various landmarks.

'That's the S.G.I.O. Building flashing the time—and see the dark snaking patch that winds around, that's the river.' He swung her around a little. 'And about there is Fig Tree Pocket where you're staying. I live over this way a bit at Jindalee.' His arm slid further around her and his warm breath fanned the side of her face. 'Mmm!' he murmured. 'Love your perfume.' His lips nuzzled her cheek and turning her in his arms he kissed her tentatively.

Bree tried not to thrust him away, not wanting to make an issue of it, but at that moment a laughing group of teenagers crossed to the fence and Alan reluctantly released her.

'Seen enough?' he asked, and when she nodded they walked back to the car.

'Didn't we come up that road?' she asked as Alan turned in the opposite direction.

'It's nice along here too,' he called back against the wind, then he eased the car into a darkened parking bay under an overhanging tree. 'Farther along that road are the four television transmitters,' he said as he switched off the engine.

'Why are we stopping here?' Bree asked nervously, shivering as the wind rustled the leaves overhead.

'Well, it's quiet and we're on our own,' said Alan, sliding his arm along the back of her seat. 'We can talk.'

'I think I'd rather go home, if you don't mind. I'm a little tired.' Bree shifted in her seat.

'Not scared of me, are you, Bree?' he asked in a teasing voice.

'Of course not! I . . . It's getting late and I think we should be heading home.'

'In a minute. It's not far from here,' Alan murmured, his fingers finding the smoothness of her neck beneath her hair. 'Has anyone ever told you you're very beautiful?' He pulled her towards him.

'Please, Alan, don't . . .'

Her words were lost as his lips covered her mouth, moved to draw a response from her, but Bree stiffened against him, trying to push him away. He only held her tighter, his lips crushing, compelling, to overcome her resistance. Fighting him only seemed to make him more determined, so she forced herself to be calm and unmoved in his hold.

But Alan mistook her passivity for encouragement and thrust his hand inside her jacket, fumbling for her breast. Agitatedly Bree tried to move his hand away, pushing against him again. He was stronger than she was and she was almost gasping for breath when he raised his head.

'Please, Alan, don't spoil our evening,' she entreated.

'Oh, come on, Bree. What's wrong with a kiss or two?' Alan was breathing heavily himself. 'Relax and enjoy it. I haven't had any complaints.' He went to kiss her again.

'No!' She turned her head away.

'Come on!' He hauled her closer, his fingers pulling at the button on her chiffon blouse. 'Don't play hard to get.'

Bree struggled away from him and the soft material tore.

'Hell!' Alan swore. 'That was your own fault. God, Bree, what's wrong with you? Anyone would think you were the original Vestal Virgin!'

Bree drew back into her seat and pulled the jacket tightly around her. 'I don't believe in necking for the sake of it.'

'Are you for real?' He stared at her as though he'd never seen her before, and she remained silent. 'Look, Bree,' he softened his tone, trying another approach,' you know I wouldn't hurt you. I've never raped any girl in my life. I just think you're a pretty great-looking bird and you turn me on. What's wrong with that? I thought you'd be flattered,' he finished woundedly.

'I am, but . . .' Bree bit her lip.

'I thought you liked me, too,' he cajoled, finding her hand and squeezing it gently.

'I do like you, Alan, and I'm sorry. I'd just like to go home now,' she told him firmly.

There was a tense silence and then Alan made a whistling sound through his teeth.

'I get it. Maybe I'm not good enough for you. You've got bigger fish to fry, is that it?'

'I don't know what you mean!' Bree tried to pull her hand away, but he held it fast.

'Oh, yes, you do. Don't play dumb.' He laughed sharply. 'Well, you can forget Heath Durant, Bree. You're flogging a dead horse.'

'Alan, that's . . .'

'Poor Bree,' he cut across her. 'Just because you're sleeping with him it doesn't mean he'll make an honest woman of you. There's no way he's going to be caught twice. He won't be played for a fool again, you take it from me.'

Bree's face had paled. 'I'm not . . . Alan, you . . . you don't know what you're saying!'

Alan shrugged. 'Don't I? I'm beginning to think I do.' He held her hand up. 'Your hand's shaking,' he said sarcastically. 'I do believe I've hit the nail on the head!'

'Alan, I've no idea what you're talking about. Now please, take me home.'

'I thought it was a bit strange you rushing off with him the other night when he snapped his fingers. Good grief, girl! Do you want money so desperately? I'll admit he's not bad looking, but he's bloody old enough to be your father!' Alan raised his voice angrily.

'He's not old.' Bree's voice broke and she gulped a steadying breath, horrified that she might have given herself away. 'I want to go home, Alan.'

'Not until I'm ready to take you,' Alan almost snarled. 'Not before I put you in the picture about your precious sugar daddy!' He grasped her arm as she fumbled for the door catch.

'I don't want to hear anything you have to say,' Bree cried.

'Well, you're going to, Miss Out-After-the-Main-Shot. Heath Durant was neatly trapped into his first marriage, so there's no way you can lure him into the same snare.'

'What . . .?' Bree swallowed, her voice caught in her throat.

'He was just a kid when he married Pamela Andrews, and he only married her because her father held a shotgun on him. She was pregnant and she said Heath Durant was responsible.'

Alan laughed. 'What a joke! He was lumbered with it.'

'How can you possibly know . . . know all this?' Bree asked, horrified at his words, his attitude.

'Because dear sweet Pamela was on with my good old dad, for one. She was almost instrumental in breaking up my parents' marriage. I can remember Mum dragging my sister and me over to our grandparents' house, and all the tears and the fights. When Pamela married Heath Dad talked Mum into coming back to him. You know—come on home, all is forgiven.'

'I'd rather you didn't tell me all this, Alan.' Bree wished she could cover her ears with her hands. 'It's none of my business.'

'God, I've just had a thought.' Alan laughed. 'Reece Durant, that's Pamela's son and whoever else's, could be my brother!'

Bree shrank away from him. 'How can you even talk about such a thing?'

Alan shrugged. 'That's life, isn't it? Anyway, it's pretty unlikely. Dad wasn't the only one. Pamela also had a thing for Ran Hailey. He was going to marry her before he found out about her affairs with my father and Heath Durant. So Ran dropped her too. That left Heath, and he fell for the bait she dangled, hook, line and sinker, with a prod from her father.'

Surely all this couldn't be true? Bree's memory flashed back to the afternoon in the garden when Ranald Hailey had mentioned Heath's wife. He had behaved in a strange withdrawn sort of manner before they were interrupted by Heath's return. And how many times had she sensed some kind of antagonism between the two men? Could it be that it all went back to their involvement with

Pamela Durant? There was apparently more to it than the simple fact that Heath had sought out and married the boss's daughter. He still could have, she told herself, but perhaps he had ended up with more than he'd bargained for.

'Did Reece know about all this?' she asked quietly.

'Who knows? People talk, so I'd say he would have been hard pressed not to have found out. I suppose you know Reece has cut out. He was always something of a delinquent.'

'Sounds as if he had just cause,' Bree remarked drily, having her first spark of sympathy for Reece. It had to have made some impression on him, that was for sure.

'From what I've heard,' Alan continued, his anger momentarily forgotten, 'Pamela and Ran continued their love-hate affair after Pamela married Heath. In fact Ran Hailey was in the car Pamela was driving the night she was killed. Seems they'd been at Ran's place and had a blazing row and were heading back to town. Of course, Heath had it hushed up. Money speaks all languages.'

Bree sat in stunned silence scarcely taking it all in, and only when Alan touched her arm did she realise he had spoken again.

'I said, isn't that right, Bree? Money speaks all languages, especially the language of love, or should I say sex?' He glared at her angrily. 'How much should I offer you, Bree?' he asked nastily, and Bree's hand snaked up to catch his face.

The sound died into the darkness and she held her stinging palm clasped in her other hand. 'Alan, take me home,' she gulped back a sob.

Alan sat immobile for a few moments before he swore and backed the car out on to the road. Even the speed he drove, exceeding the limits, couldn't seem to penetrate Bree's numbed consciousness. She was lost in herself, her mind mulling over and over what Alan had told her and its connotations.

If half of it was true it was a sordid story. Her heart went out to Heath. Was it any wonder his attitude was coldly cynical before anything else? After what had happened to him when he would have been about eighteen years old she would hardly be able to convince him that she loved him purely and simply as a woman for a man. When he found out she had lied to him he would be even less inclined to trust her. No matter which way she turned it would all come back to that lie about Ben. She was neatly caught in a trap of her own making.

At all costs ... Oh, God! Bree's hand clutched at her heart as the final telling stroke cut through her. The chance that Reece wasn't Heath's responsibility, that Heath should be under no obligation at all where Reece's son was concerned. In all fairness ... Bree's thoughts were catapulted back to the present as Alan switched off the engine of the M.G.

Realising they were in front of Heath's house, she pulled her scarf from her head. The house was in darkness save for the glow of the outside patio light that Peg had left for Bree before the Rolands had retired. As she went to climb out of the car Alan put his hand lightly on her arm.

'Bree, please. Wait a minute.' he began, and she turned back to him. 'Look, I'm sorry. I was way out of line and I had no right to say what I did.' He sighed ruefully. 'I behaved like a frustrated fool, I guess. Will you accept my apology?'

Still in a state of shock as Alan's revelations

spun about inside her, Bree could only nod, and he squeezed her hand.

'Thanks, Bree. Although I have a feeling I may have spoiled any future between us I'd sure as hell like you to tell me I haven't.' His eyes appealed to her in the circle of light from the patio.

'I don't know, Alan. Let's leave it for the moment. I think I'd better go in.' Bree opened the door of the car. 'But thanks for the beautiful dinner.'

'Okay.' Reluctantly he released her hand. 'Can I ring you again some time?'

'If you like.' Bree didn't look at him as she climbed out of the car. She'd made up her mind. By the time Alan phoned she'd be long gone. No wonder she had seen no resemblance between Heath and Reece! If what Alan said was true it was totally unfair for Heath to be under any obligation to Reece's son. She couldn't stay here, living so close to Heath, at his expense, knowing they had no right to do so.

Turning slowly as the red spots of Alan's M.G.'s tail-lights disappeared around the curve of the drive, Bree stepped shakily to the door, her trembling fingers all thumbs as she fumbled for the key. Suddenly the door was wrenched open and a tall broad figure stood vaguely outlined in the darkness beyond. Her hand flew to her mouth, her bag falling to the floor.

'Heath!' she breathed as he stepped into the circle of light and bent to retrieve her bag, handing it back to her. 'What . . .? When . . .?'

He raised one sardonic eyebrow, the planes and angles of his face set and forbidding as he stood back for her to enter.

'I take it you mean what am I doing here and

when did I get back?' he said mockingly as he
flicked on the living-room lights and closed the
door with a subdued click. 'To the first, I'm here
because it's still my home, and to the second,
about,' he glanced down at his wristwatch, 'three
hours ago.'

'Oh.' Bree stood staring at him, the cold anger
that exuded from him making her heart beat in her
throat. 'Peg said you weren't expected back
tonight.'

'Obviously. You didn't waste much time making
alterative arrangements for this evening,' he
remarked clippedly.

'Alternative . . .? But Alan said . . .' Bree
stopped. What exactly had Alan said? Only that
he'd taken over Heath's restaurant booking. And
she had surmised that Heath knew, had wanted to
show her how easily he could fob her off on
someone else. 'I thought you knew.' She lifted her
head to face him levelly.

Heath leant back against the door and folded
his arms. He had shed his jacket, but he still wore
the waistcoat of his dark three-piece suit and his
shirt was unbuttoned at the collar.

'Alan said he'd taken over your dinner
booking,' Bree explained. 'At the Fountain Room.'

Heath straightened up. 'I haven't seen or spoken
to young Paine since last night. How the hell
would he know where I'd planned to take you to
dinner?'

'I don't know. I naturally thought you'd told
him to take me instead of yourself. That's why I
went.' Bree's voice trembled and she felt close to
tears as his eyes raked her, his expression not
giving her the impression that he believed her at
all. 'That's the truth.'

'You took a long time over dinner. Did you enjoy yourself?' he asked flatly.

'It was all right.' Her eyes faltered from the cynical twist of his lips.

'Sounds like a fun evening.'

'I don't see any point in discussing it tonight.' He couldn't have made his scepticism plainer. Bree shrugged nervously out of Peg's jacket as she turned away from him. 'It's late. I'm tired and I'm going to bed.'

'Seems like we've been through all this before.' His fingers grabbed her arm and swung her back to face him. 'Well, I haven't finished discussing it, not by a long chalk,' he bit out through clenched teeth. 'But I can't really see talking accomplishing anything between us, can you?'

His lips were crushing hers before she could catch her breath, his mouth plundering, and even knowing his driving anger Bree was powerless to suppress her automatic response. Heath raised his head and held her slightly away from him.

'I've been sitting here for three hours imagining you with that young pup, trying to devise some means of punishing you for going with him tonight,' he said with biting chilliness.

'Heath, that's not fair! I told you Alan implied you knew about his intention to take me out. I thought you'd—well, suggested it.' Her fingers felt tremblingly for the button on her chiffon blouse before she remembered the blouse was torn, and she was far too slow to hide it from Heath's sharp eyes.

One hand left her shoulder to dart down to grasp the ragged material in his fingers. His lips thinned.

'How did that happen?' he asked quietly.

Her eyes fell away from his. 'I caught it on . . . on something.'

'Don't lie to me, Bree!' His voice was now ominously even.

'It was nothing—honestly. It was accidental,' she blurted out.

'I'll bet it was!' He shook her, her hair cascading forward over her face and she pushed one side nervously back behind her ear. 'What the hell did he do to you?' he demanded. 'Tell me, Bree, or I'll . . .'

'Or you'll what?' she threw out at him in a surge of sudden anger, the whole distressful evening catching up with her. 'What will you do, Heath? Make the situation worse than it already is by gallantly calling him out over it?'

'Bree, I asked you a question.' He was white about the mouth, his jaw set aggressively.

'Well, the answer is he simply tried to do what you were doing a minute ago. He tried to kiss me and I wouldn't play. Now are you satisfied?' She heard her voice echoing shrilly and drew a steadying breath. 'And I don't need you to start beating your chest and going all protective, because I can take care of myself. I'm not going to let myself be used, not by Alan Paine and not by you. Now, let me go! Because I don't think I can take any more tonight.'

She broke out of his hold and bolted for her room, locking the door after her.

CHAPTER ELEVEN

AT some stage during that sleepless night Bree decided she had to leave at once. Not only because of the doubtfulness of Ben's relationship to Heath but because she knew it was only time before her traitorous body succumbed to Heath's magnetic assault. Then everything would be lost without redemption.

Recalling her feelings when Alan kissed her only proved what she already knew, that whatever and whoever came after, nothing, no one could bring her alive the way Heath could. If he had followed her last night she would have had no defence against him.

She was deeply in love with him, loved him with every last fibre of her being, but she very much doubted he could offer her such a full and complete commitment. He wanted her physically, she couldn't dispute that, and she would be useful while he was attracted to her, but she couldn't bear to see his interest begin to wane. She would simply have to steal quietly away, go somewhere where he would never find her, and try to forget him.

For a couple of days she plotted, heavy-hearted, formulating plans and discarding them, keeping well out of Heath's way. As she had barely seen him since that night she could only believe he was of the same mind and had no desire to seek her out. She told herself she was profoundly thankful when he was urgently summoned to Cairns in north Queensland.

Her chance to make her escape came two days after Heath's departure. Noticing her pallor and heavy eyes, Peg had rarely left her on her own and she couldn't bring herself to baldly state her decision to leave. At any rate, she could never totally count on Peg not calling Heath immediately if she so much as suspected Bree's intention.

'Bill and I have been promising our daughter we'll go over and spend a few days with her and her family,' Peg told her that morning, 'and with Heath away for what may be a week it's such a good opportunity.'

'That's a great idea,' Bree filled her voice with enthusiasm, her stomach churning nervously.

'Yes. But I'll worry about you here on your own, so why don't you and the baby come with us. My daughter would love to meet you, and there's plenty of room,' Peg suggested.

'But I don't mind being here alone,' Bree began.

'I know. But you've been looking so peaky, love, I'm sure the change would do you the world of good, wouldn't it, Bill?' she appealed to her husband.

'Stop bullying the girl, Peg.' Bill smiled at Bree. 'She might be better off for a rest from your chatter-chatter!'

Bree laughed with him at Peg's indignant expression. 'Honestly, Peg, I would rather stay here. You and Bill go by yourselves, and have a good time.' She forced a lightness into her voice. 'Besides, I've still got that book I borrowed from you to finish.'

Eventually Peg was convinced, and tears blinded Bree's eyes as she watched the Rolands drive away. In the short time she had been here Peg and Bill had shown her nothing but kindness, and she felt dreadful as she penned an inadequate note of apology and thanks to them.

She had hurriedly packed her clothes and Ben's, leaving all the beautiful outfits from the boutique hanging in the huge closet. It was bad enough that she had to turn thief without taking the clothes as well. With only a little over a hundred dollars to her name she had taken two hundred dollars from Heath's desk, assuring him in the note she left until the last minute to write that she would pay him the money back as soon as she could.

Reading the note through before she sealed it in an envelope brought the choking tears back. It seemed so trite and said nothing of her feelings, but if she'd tried to put any of it on paper she knew she would have lost the courage to leave. And when the taxi arrived she climbed inside without allowing herself a backward glance.

The Greyhound Bus depot was alive now with comings and goings, and Bree sat with a sleeping Ben on her lap watching people arriving from or departing for various parts of Australia. It felt as though she had been sitting here for ever, but in fact it was only long enough for her to have purchased her ticket and given Ben his orange juice. In another half an hour their bus would be off, and she wished the time would fly by so that she could be away from here. And away from Heath.

There was nothing for her back in Bundaberg, but she had to go somewhere, and at least she could ask the girls she had shared a house with if they could put her up until she found somewhere to board. Perhaps she could get work as a live-in-housekeeper.

Bree sighed, swallowing the tears that threatened to choke her, and glanced down at Ben as he slept peacefully. It was going to be hard to start again, especially when she was leaving her heart here, but for Ben's sake she had to do it. When you had the responsibility of an innocent child you had no choice.

The doors opened and a pair of long grey-clad legs moved into the depot with precise purposeful strides, paused and crossed to halt in front of her. Slowly Bree's eyes slid upwards. His expensive pale blue shirt was slightly dishevelled, the buttons partially undone, and a streak of dirt marred one long sleeve.

Her heartbeats felt as though they literally stopped as she gazed into his face. His eyes were red rimmed and his hair fell forward on to his forehead and the lines on either side of his mouth seemed to be etched much deeper. He was so far removed from the immaculately dressed business man that Bree could only gaze speechlessly up at him, her mouth dry with shock.

Without uttering a word Heath bent down and picked up her battered suitcase, his other hand clasping her arm, pulling her to her feet, walking her to the door.

The red Ferrari was waiting arrogantly in a no-parking zone and he threw her case into the boot and held the passenger side door open for Bree to climb inside. She didn't even attempt to break away from him. Her rubbery legs would have been incapable of carrying her.

Heath pulled from the kerb into the traffic and she glanced sideways at him, scarcely believing he was there.

'How did you know where to find me?' Her voice was little better than a whisper.

'I have influential friends,' he replied cynically.

Ill at ease, Bree looked from his set profile to the streak of dirt on his shirt sleeve and then to his hands on the steering wheel, catching her breath at the sight of the raw scrape across his knuckles.

'Your hand—what happened?' she asked, snatching her own hand back as she went involuntarily to touch him.

'I had a slight altercation with a certain party.'

'With . . .' Bree blinked incredulously. 'You mean you had a fight with someone?'

'I prefer slight altercation,' he remarked drily.

'Who . . . with?'

'Does it matter?' he shrugged.

'You went after Alan?' she suggested, and Heath laughed harshly.

'I caught up with your friend Paine, yes, but not for the reasons you're imagining.'

'Heath, please, what's going on? Who did you have this fight with? And why?'

'I arrived home earlier this afternoon and I found your note,' he told her flatly, and when she made no comment he shot a glance at her. 'I rather thought young Paine might know where you'd gone.'

'And you hit him?'

'No. There was no need. He was quite loquacious and happy to be able to tell me he had no idea of your whereabouts. But he could clear up one or two interesting mysteries. It seems I underestimated my long-standing friend Ran Hailey,' Heath's voice dropped icily.

'Ran Hailey?' Bree frowned.

'He was in my office the day I was called away urgently to the site in Toowoomba. He heard me cancel my dinner reservations at the Fountain Room and couldn't get to young Paine fast enough to thrust a spoke in my wheel.'

'Why . . . why would he want to do that?'

'Because Ran Hailey has let an old feud fester on inside him for nearly twenty years, he's fed off it, dug away at me and never forgotten. I always suspected he worked on Reece's problems to cause more trouble, and from what Paine told me I suspected he might have had a hand in your disappearance.'

'I haven't seen Ranald Hailey since the party,' Bree told him.

'I know.' His jaw tightened. 'But he had a hard time convincing me.'

'You mean you fought with Ranald Hailey? Over . . .' Bree swallowed, and her face washed with colour. 'What did you fight about?'

'You,' he said without expression, although his eyes smouldered with feeling. 'And other things that should have been long buried and forgotten.'

'But Ranald Hailey couldn't have told you where to find me.' Bree wouldn't allow herself to compute the underlying message in the blue gaze he had turned on her.

'No. He eventually persuaded me that he didn't, so I rang a friend who has access to the taxi companies. It wasn't hard to find the driver who picked you up.' One corner of his mouth lifted ironically. 'Only time-consuming.'

Bree sat in silence then, her stomach churning at the thought of Heath Durant going to such lengths to find her. And why had he brought her back?

'You've led me a merry dance, Bree,' he said softly. 'Bree. It's an unusual name, isn't it?' His tone was so deceptively casual and Bree swallowed with nervous guilt.

'Yes. Yes, it is,' she said uneasily.

Heath moved to flick on the headlights, for it was growing dark now, and neither of them spoke until he drew up in front of the house Bree had been so sure she would never see again.

'You'd better settle the baby,' said Heath when they were inside and he had flooded the room with light. 'I need a shower and a shave.' He unbuttoned the cuffs of his shirt, his face turned away from her.

'Heath, I . . .' Bree began shakily, and he glanced at her then, the lines of tiredness evident in his stance.

'Later, Bree,' he said flatly. 'I came straight here from the airport and I'd like to change. We'll talk then.' His eyes moved over her but she could gauge nothing from his expression. 'We have a lot to talk about,' he added ominously as he strode from the room.

She'd have to tell him, she decided, biting her lip, her hands going to her stomach as it twisted uptightly. Now that Ben was tucked back into his cot she had to face Heath and she was filled with dread. She showered and changed, choosing one of her new outfits, a soft pale grey jumpsuit, because she needed the confidence it gave her, for she knew it would take every last ounce of her courage to try to explain the whole mixed-up mess.

He was waiting for her in the living-room, standing by the bar with an untouched drink in his hand. He had changed into dark brown slacks and a light cream sweatshirt, the tie laces at the neck undone, and his hair was a shade darker, still damp from his shower. Bree's heart constricted in her breast as she looked at him and the pain of loving him ached deep within her.

'Would you like something to drink?' he asked,

his eyes on his own glass now, after giving her one all-encompassing glance as she had entered the living-room.

'No, thank you.' She shook her head and took a deep breath. 'Heath, I ... There's something I have to tell you. I ... I'm not ...' She swallowed, her courage faltering, so afraid of his reaction, his rejection. 'I'm not ...'

'You're not Briony Maree Ransome,' he finished, and took a sip of his drink.

'You know?' she breathed. 'How ... how could you know?'

'We'll come to that later,' he replied flatly as he turned to set his glass on the bar-top and began to walk slowly across the room towards her.

Bree was paralysed, glued to the spot, and he stopped in front of her, an arm's length, an ocean, away from her.

'You stole something from me,' he said calmly.

'I only borrowed the money. Please believe me,' she appealed to him, her hands feeling clammy from her nervousness. 'I was going to pay it back, I promise you.'

'I wasn't talking about the money. It was far more precious than that.' She felt his eyes on her, touching her, but couldn't bring herself to meet his gaze. 'You stole my heart, and I'm damned if I want it back.'

He stepped closer to her. 'Bree.' He said the name softly, a breath caress, and his finger lifted her chin until her smoky grey eyes, wide now, met the deep incredible blue of his. 'Who are you, I wonder?' he asked almost to himself, and Bree could only stare up at him as the fire in his eyes sparked the tinder-dry tension trapped between them.

His arms crushed her to him and beneath her

hands splayed out on his chest she could feel her
own heart's thudding echo in his. His lips moved
against the curve of her neck and his breath teased
the nerve endings around her ear.

'When I found out you'd lied to me I was so
blazingly angry I could have ...' he drew a
shuddering breath. 'But when I came home and
found you'd gone I thought I'd lose my mind.' His
lips slid along her jawline, found her mouth, and
they clung together caught in a flame of mutual
emotion.

'God, Bree!' he muttered huskily as his lips
surrendered hers. 'I don't give a damn who you
are. If you were the devil's child I could no more
let you go now than I could fly. God knows, I'd
cease living.'

'Oh, Heath!' Tears coursed down her cheeks and
her arms slid around his waist as she buried her
face in his shirt.

They stood like that until her tears subsided and
she raised her head to look up at him. 'I didn't lie
about my name,' she said. 'I really am Bree
Ransome—Briane Ransome, actually. Briony's my
sister.'

A flicker of pain crossed his face and he led her
across to the lounge chair, pulling her down on to
his lap.

'Ben's my nephew. Reece and Briony left him
with me. They couldn't cope with having the baby,
so ...' She bit her lip. 'Heath, I'm sorry I didn't
tell you everything in the beginning, but I thought
you'd take him away from me, and he was all the
family I had left when Briony went. I didn't know
then about Reece not being ...' She stopped, and
Heath raised his eyebrow.

'Alan told me that Reece wasn't your son and I

couldn't let you take the responsibility for Ben when ... if that was so.' She looked up at him, expecting anger but finding only a cynical resignation.

'Old stories linger on, don't they?' he said tiredly, his hand moving caressingly on her arm.

'Is it true?'

'It was all a long time ago,' he sighed. 'Although I can't understand what interest young Paine could have in the story.'

'The night I went out with Alan he thought that because I didn't want him kissing me, that I was ... that you and I were ... involved.'

Heath's eyes smouldered, sending shivers of pure sensuality down her spine.

'Involved!' he gave a soft laugh. 'I somehow think you and I have been involved, for want of a better word, since the night we met. I knew the moment I put my arms around you that there was no way I could ever let you go.'

'I felt it, too,' Bree admitted, her heart beating wildly in her breast. 'I was so confused. Nothing like that had ever happened to me before. You were so ...' She gave an embarrassed laugh and Heath raised his eyebrows mockingly.

'So?' he prompted.

'So handsome and unlike anyone I'd ever known before in my life. And so far apart from the life I've been used to that I couldn't see any future in—well, hoping you might feel the same way. You seemed so distant and almost angry that night at the flat.'

'I was eaten up by pure unadulterated jealousy.' He shook his head slowly. 'When I imagined you had a child, that you belonged to some other man, it was bad enough, but when it turned out to be my own son I couldn't believe the pain that knowledge caused me.'

'There was never anything between Reece and myself. I've never . . .' Bree stopped and warmth coloured her cheeks. 'I've never been with anyone.'

'Oh, Bree!' he sighed, carrying her hand to his lips and gently kissing the softness of her palm.

'Then Reece is your son?' Bree asked him quietly.

'I've always accepted him as my son,' he replied. 'When Pamela told me she was pregnant I believed I was responsible. I was disgusted with myself for letting it happen. I owed her father so much, and to repay him like that—well, I wasn't proud of myself. I can't pretend I was in love with her, but Jack Andrews was a sick man, so Pamela and I were married.'

'Ran Hailey said she was very beautiful,' Bree said, and then wished she hadn't as his jaw tightened.

'Yes, she was beautiful,' he agreed, 'but it was only skin-deep, believe me. After we were married when things didn't go her way she began to toss insinuations at me about her involvement with other men, mostly Ran Hailey, and it didn't take long for our relationship to shrivel up and die. I threw myself into the business and Pamela went her own way. She was with Ran Hailey when her car left the road near his place. She was killed instantly.'

'What about Reece?'

'Unfortunately Reece was caught up in the middle and I was so absorbed in my work that I didn't realise what it was doing to him until it was too late.' He rubbed a weary hand across his eyes. 'So you see, I've got no great track record when it comes to being a model husband and father.' His eyes roved over her face with a brooding intensity. 'I guess I've got a colossal nerve asking you to take a chance on me,' he admitted honestly.

'Oh, Heath, I love you so much it would be no chance at all. I was dying inside, leaving today.'

'God knows, I love you, too.' He held her to him. 'And I'm selfish enough to not want to let you go.'

'Can you forgive me for not telling you the truth about myself and about Reece and Briony?' she asked, and he looked even more strained and drawn. 'Heath?'

'There's nothing to forgive. You did what you thought was best for the child. No one could blame you for that.' He sighed. 'But about your sister and Reece—they're in Cairns.'

Bree frowned, sensing his disquiet. 'You found them?'

He nodded. 'I was called to Cairns by the police because they had Reece in custody. It seems he's suspected of being involved in drug trafficking on the Tableland.'

'Drugs?' Bree was flabbergasted. 'But Reece despised anyone who took drugs! Surely he couldn't have had anything to do with that sort of thing?'

'He said he wasn't involved.' Heath ran a hand through his hair. 'He had the police phone me to bail him out. I flew straight up there intending to sort him out, about the drug thing and about his responsibilities.' He grimaced and Bree slid her hand sympathetically along the side of his face. 'I failed again. He thanked me reluctantly for the bail money and when I reminded him about his son he told me, and I quote, to go to hell, that he wanted no ties and neither did Briony.'

'Oh, Heath, I'm sorry!'

His fingers covered hers, and he turned his head so that his lips found her palm.

'You saw Briony?' Bree asked, and he shook his head.

'No—at least, not to talk to. A young girl collected Reece after he'd been released, but by then Reece and I had said all he'd wanted said. So,' he shrugged unhappily, 'stalemate again.'

'Heath, what about Ben?'

'We'll adopt him legally, and maybe give him some brothers and sisters,' he smiled at her then, a promise in his eyes. 'Perhaps I can make a better job with him than I did with his father, with your help.' He looked at her levelly. 'Will you marry me, Bree, knowing what you'll be taking on? A cynical old man and a ready-made family!'

'You're not an old man,' she said indignantly, 'and I've always felt more like Ben's mother than his aunt.' She smiled tremulously. 'I love you so much I think I'd stay with you on any terms,' she whispered.

'I can't live without you, Bree. That's something I've never said to any woman. It's marriage or nothing, I wouldn't ask anything else of you, my love,' he said reverently, and his lips met hers gently, all anger gone, in a kiss that sealed their future. 'At least this time our children will know how much I adore their mother.'

Some time later Heath gave a soft laugh. 'Peg's going to be ecstatic about this! For years she's been suggesting I'd be so much better off if I was married. What time are they expected home?'

'They've gone to their daughter's for a couple of days.' Bree blushed as his eyes narrowed.

'You mean we're on our own?'

Bree nodded. 'There's only you and me. And Ben.'

'Then I think I'm going to have to cut some thick red tape to get the fastest marriage licence on record,' he said huskily.

'And until then?' Bree ran her fingers inside the collar of his shirt, exalting in the firm smoothness of his skin.

'Bree, don't look at me like that!' Heath groaned. 'I'm a very fallible man at the moment. My resistance is at a low ebb with you so close to me, and I want you to have everything the way it should be, the wedding, a honeymoon. I want it to be perfect for you.'

Bree snuggled closer, nuzzling soft kisses along the line of his jaw. 'I love you, Heath, and knowing you love me, too—well, nothing could ever make my life more perfect.'